MY NAME IS APHRODITE

Wings Press, Inc.

Vera Berry Burrows

My Name is Aphrodite

"A monastery? Why would we go to a monastery, Jake? It's madness."

Jake was thoughtful. "Think about it, Rodi. When Cory Demetriou lost his father, and his mother and sister had disappeared without a trace, he might have found it necessary to withdraw from the world. It would be a lot for a young man to take," he explained. "I do know that many Greek people go on pilgrimages to Mount Athos, but no females are allowed to go in the monasteries."

"So why are we going?" Rodi asked, totally confused by the way things were turning out. "The whole thing makes me feel uncomfortable with the thought that my father might have become a monk. How would I deal with that, Jake? How would *he* deal with the fact that he has a daughter? I almost feel like giving up."

"You can't give up," Jake interrupted. "If Roussos is telling the truth and we find him at Mount Athos, we'll decide then what to say and do. At least you will meet him and fulfil your mum's request."

"How can I meet him if no women are allowed there?" Rodi cried in desperation.

"I'll go and make enquiries first," Jake suggested, "and then if he's there, I'll request that he obtain a pass to come and meet you. They must have something in place for such eventualities."

"That's if he wants to," Rodi said. "Oh Jake, I feel so helpless." Tears began to flow again and Jake held her close to show his support, his affection and his unwavering love.

MY NAME IS
APHRODITE

Vera Berry Burrows

Wings ePress, Inc.

Edited by: Jeanne R. Smith
Copy Edited by: Joan C. Powell
Senior Editor: Jeanne R. Smith
Executive Editor: Marilyn Kapp
Cover Artist: Trisha FitzGerald

All rights reserved

Wings ePress Books
http://www.wingsepress.com

Copyright © 2014 Vera Berry Burrows
ISBN 978-1-61309-813-4

Published In the United States Of America

Wings ePress Inc.
3000 N. Rock Road
Newton, KS 67114

Dedication

This is for all my friends in Australia. Thank you for helping me to make Australia home.

One

1959

Adele Bartlett was sixteen years old when she fell pregnant and the father of her child seemed to have disappeared. Her only way of finding him was to contact the manager of the Greek hotel where he worked. "He is a grown man," the hotel manager informed Adele when she enquired as to his whereabouts. "He has moved on and we don't know where he has gone. We cannot supply you with information about him. If you are accusing him of some crime against you, then you must involve the police."

"Oh nothing like that," Adele had said at the time. Consensual sex was not a crime. She had known exactly what she was doing.

~ * ~

1981

Rodi Bartlett sat on the plane taking her to the land of her conception. She couldn't call it the land of her birth since her sixteen year old mother had flown back to England at the end of the annual two weeks in the sun in August nineteen-fifty-nine unaware that she was pregnant. A twenty-one year old Greek man had no idea he had sown the seed of her future. Since the story had been exposed in her mother, Adele's, will, he had never been told of her existence. *Why should he?* Adele had written in the exposé. *English girls on holiday on the romantic island of Corfu never considered the consequences of holiday flings...*but Rodi's mother had apparently never regarded the situation as simply a holiday romance. *For me, it was the time I fell hopelessly in love; the only time I had been so completely in love. The handsome hotel receptionist probably had hundreds of holiday romances every summer so why would I be any different from the others?*

Now at the age of twenty-one herself, her mother prematurely dead from the most dreaded of diseases for which nobody had yet found a cure, Rodi was going in search of the father who had never been discussed, but whose name had finally been revealed in a codicil to her mother's will. Rodi took the document out of her handbag and re-read it for the umpteenth time: *My dearest wish is that my daughter, Aphrodite (Rodi by her own volition) finds her father, Cory Demetriou, last known to me at the Hotel Helenya, near Paleokastritsa on the island of Corfu in August 1959. She has the right to know him as I never did. There is no animosity; I fell in love with him when I was on holiday. I have no regrets and she has been the perfect daughter, but I owe it to her to allow her to know her father and hopefully discover the handsome, charming and caring man I met and loved albeit for a very short time. Kalí týchi, Rodi. Good luck.*

Rodi opened the five year diary she had started at the beginning of the year. *I must keep a record of this journey,* she thought. *Whatever the outcome, I need to be able to look back and know that I did my best.*

As the plane touched down in Corfu, Rodi experienced a feeling of *déjà vu*. Although she had never been to Greece, she found a sort of affiliation to it and there was something quite compelling about the island of Corfu. Her mother had said very little about it, only that it was lovely and it was the one and only time she had gone overseas on holiday.

"It was very beautiful, Aphrodite..."

"Rodi, please Mum. I really love my name because it's unusual, but kids at school don't understand why it's different and I'm tired of explaining to them." She had always insisted on the shortened version.

I wish Mum had told me about Cory Demetriou, she thought again as she waited to collect her luggage. She had gone over and over it in her mind, but it was impossible to find the answers she needed. *Maybe she preferred to forget, but I hope she wasn't sad because of having loved and lost. Dear Mum...she protected me all my life from the details of my father. I'm sad about that. I wonder if she were ashamed? She told me that my name came from her love of Greek mythology.* She shivered involuntarily. *I never even knew my father was Greek. She only ever told me that she had fallen in love—once—and I was the product of that love. When I asked where my father was, she always said she didn't know and asked me not to talk about him. Out of love and respect for her, I did as she asked, but now, how I wish I knew the whole story.*

~ * ~

Summer 1959

Adele Bartlett had saved for a whole year so that she might go on holiday with her friend; no parents, no adults to spoil their fun. Not only was it her first holiday without her parents, it was her first trip abroad; her first flight in an aeroplane; her first adventure in a country where she couldn't speak the language.

"How will we know what to ask for in shops?" she asked her best friend. "I can hardly pronounce the name of the place where we're staying."

Eva Chesterton laughed. "Stop worrying, Adie. You'll be fine and it's Paleo...cas...tritsa," she emphasised.

"That's all right for you to say," Adele stated strongly, but not grudgingly. "You've had rich parents to take you abroad every year since you were in nappies. For girls like me, even going to Skegness in the pouring rain was a treat!"

"Now you're being melodramatic, Adele, so stop it," her friend said gently. "You are the best friend I have and I wouldn't change that for all the money in the world. My parents aren't really rich, but I appreciate that I only have to ask and I usually get. Mind you, I haven't asked for a Ferrari yet!" She grinned and nudged her friend playfully.

"Exactly, and I really love you for being my friend. There are other girls in our school who look down their noses at people like me."

"Oh Adie, I know who you mean and Nancy Prior has no real friends, so don't worry about her," Eva reassured her. "I know for a fact your dad and stepmum give you everything they think you need. They always make me feel welcome and I just love your dad's sense of humour. He should go on the stage, but having said that, I doubt if your mum would allow it. Anyway, there's no stigma in not having a lot of money, especially when what you have is earned in an honest and hard-working way."

"I know that, Eva, but you're right, my mum would never lower herself to be known as a comedian's wife!" She had to laugh. "Dad said when my real mum passed away when she had me, Ivy took charge and helped him through his grief. She's been all right, but I have never really been close to her, even though she's always been there and I have called her Mum all my life.

Dad only told me the truth when I was twelve. I often think she resents me being so close to my dad, but I am very conscious of the fact that she does have a very high opinion of herself at times and doesn't seem to move with the times. I could never explain the..." She paused to choose her words carefully. She took a deep breath before she continued. "...the feeling of envy I had every August when you left for Spain or France or any of the other hot places you flew off to every year and Mum told me Skegness had always been good enough for her, so it should be good enough for me. Still, here I am flying off to Corfu..."

Eva linked her arm through Adele's and squeezed her hand as the plane took off from East Midlands Airport, next stop Corfu. Adele tensed as she felt the aircraft leave the ground, but dozed on and off between the snacks of nuts and cheese and biscuits as well as what she could only describe as a compact—not compacted—meal of chicken, hard carrots, potato rosti and some sort of sauce the flavour of which she didn't recognise. She picked at the chicken and sampled the rosti, but didn't eat it all.

"Not exactly *cordon bleu*, is it?" Eva commented, "But don't worry. We'll make up for it with all the Greek food we'll sample during the next two weeks."

Adele wasn't so sure. "That's something else I'm worried about. What if I don't like *moussaka, tzatziki, taramosolata* and *souvlaki*?" she asked plaintively. "I looked up Greek food in a book at the library. My mum would never make anything like that. She's a meat and three veg person through and through. Mind you, I like the sound of the desserts. *Baklava* and *loukoumi* sound yummy." She grinned. "If I live off sugar desserts for two weeks, I'll go back home the size of a bus!"

When they landed in Corfu, there was a mad rush to block up the aisle and retrieve hand luggage that had been stored in the overhead lockers. Eva didn't move. Adele looked at her in panic. "Come on, Eva. Everybody will get off the plane before us..."

"Calm down, Adie. This always happens. They still have to wait for their luggage to be unloaded so they won't gain any time at all by pushing and shoving their way off the plane," Eva told her. "Trust me." She giggled, showing she was still just a young girl going on holiday without her parents in spite of being a seasoned traveller. "We have two whole weeks to get the best tan ever."

The heat hit them as soon as they reached the exit. "Wow!" was all Adele could say. As she looked up at the cloudless azure sky, she thrilled with excitement and they hurried to arrivals to wait for their luggage. After they had retrieved it, the coach trip to the hotel seemed to take forever. There was no air conditioning in the vehicle and the air that blew in through open windows was hot and dry. The bus literally rattled along the winding, dusty tracks. She nervously hung on to the handle on the seat in front of her and stared out across the barren landscape until suddenly she was confronted by lots of green trees: tall cypresses and later olive trees bedecked with huge nets to collect the olives at harvest time. Still the tracks remained the same, but eventually, they turned into huge ornate gates where the road became level, tarmacked and bordered with beautiful bougainvillea that led them to the Hotel Helenya, their home for the next two weeks.

"This is absolutely luxurious, Eva," Adele said as they climbed the marble steps into the reception area of the hotel. "It's hard to believe that after driving along those rough roads, something as beautiful as this has been built in the perfect spot. Just look at the blue sea!" she exclaimed. "I have never seen anything like it. The North Sea at Skegness is always murky grey even when the sun is shining!"

Eva smiled and squeezed Adele's arm. "I knew you'd like it," she said.

"Like it?" Adele replied happily. "I love it and I've only just arrived. Oh Eva, thanks for bringing me. I can't believe I'm actually in Corfu and..."

"Do you have your passports, ladies?" the receptionist interrupted in impeccable English which surprised Adele. She smiled at him and Eva, deliberately grinning, nudged her.

"What?" Adele asked innocently.

"Tell you later," she whispered. "Will you please keep our passports in the safe?" she asked the receptionist.

He nodded. "Certainly, madam. Your room is four-two-five, twin room with en suite and sea view. Enjoy your holiday."

When they were in the elevator, Adele confronted her friend, not very aggressively, but more out of bewildered curiosity. "Why did you nudge me?" she asked, "and why did you let him keep our passports? I've never had a passport and I don't want to forget it when I leave, otherwise they might not let me back into England. My dad and mum would be devastated! It took me a whole year just to get them to agree to this holiday. They kept coming up with all sorts of things that might happen to me while I'm here— food poisoning, sunstroke, mosquito bites, you name it, it is all going to happen to me!" She had to laugh at herself for even relating all that to Eva.

Eva laughed with her. "We'll be fine, Adie. Here we are, fourth floor. Come on. We'll unpack and have a walk round afterwards to get our bearings."

"But you still haven't told me why you nudged me," Adele said.

Eva grinned. "Smiling like that at a young Greek man would suggest you were flirting with him."

"I wasn't!" she exclaimed. "I was just so pleased he could speak such good English."

"I know that," Eva told her, "but I'm not sure he did. Here's our room. Did you pick up the key?"

Adele held out the tiny key on an absolutely massive key ring. "They don't intend us losing this, do they? It looks like a prison cell key!"

They both laughed again. "No way!" Eva said happily. "We are free! We are free! Two whole weeks without adult interference! Corfu, here we come!"

The first few days were spent literally lying in the sun all day by the pool. Intermittently, the girls would dive in the pool for a swim and cool down and then apply copious amounts of Ambre Solaire to prevent burning, but the first night both were bright red and on fire!

"I can't sleep," Adele complained. "I'm red hot!"

"Just lie on top of the bed and you'll feel better," Eva told her. "I'm hot too even though I used almost a full bottle of suntan lotion."

"I did too, Eva. I didn't realise getting a tan was so uncomfortable."

"You'll be fine, Adie. Tomorrow the red will begin to turn into a beautiful golden colour and you'll look really fabulous."

"I certainly hope so," Adele replied.

"You'll wow all the boys, I'm telling you! I saw those Scottish boys eyeing you up this afternoon. One of them is really good looking."

"Stop it, Eva," Adele snapped. "I don't want a Scottish boy or any other boy, thank you very much. I have Gary at home. I promised him I wouldn't get off with anybody while I'm here."

Eva sighed. "Everybody has holiday romances, Adele," she said matter-of-factly. "They don't mean anything. It's just makes you feel good that a guy fancies you and you can flirt outrageously for a couple of weeks."

Adele shrugged. "Not interested. I want to get a tan, sample the food, see the sights..."

"Exactly," Eva interjected. "And some of the sights are all the handsome guys!"

"Stop it, Eva!" Adele demanded, but had to laugh with her friend.

"They sure are sexy though," Eva said dreamily.

Adele gasped. "Behave, Eva!" she exclaimed. "Sexy doesn't come into it." She paused significantly and then said very seriously, "I've never done it. Have you?"

Eva looked sheepish.

"You have, haven't you?" Adele was shocked. "Who with? You naughty girl! I'm saving myself for my dream man and I'm not likely to meet him here in just two weeks. I wouldn't have time to know if he's my Mr Right in such a short time." She eyed Eva curiously and then, "What was it like?" she asked with a shy smile.

Eva adjusted her baby-doll pyjamas and sat cross-legged on her bed. She faced Adele and took a deep breath. "Well..."

"Come on, don't be shy," Adele coaxed "You've been encouraging me to spread my wings a bit ever since we arrived here, so come on, tell me all."

Eva made herself feel comfortable physically and emotionally. Since Adele had broached the subject of sex, she would at last be able to tell her secret. "It wasn't enjoyable at all."

Adele looked quizzically at her and Eva continued. "I shouldn't have done it. I was only fifteen and that's why I've never told you. The boy could still be in serious trouble if I told on him and I wouldn't wish anything like that for him. He's still a nice boy and we both regret what we did."

"Don't tell me if you'd prefer not to," Adele told her. "It really doesn't matter and I won't say anything more about it—promise."

Eva shook her head. "I'd rather tell you, Adie. I've kept the secret a whole year and I trust you. I was in Paris last yearwith my parents. My dad's business partner, Xavier Bresson, lives there. Monsieur and Madame Bresson have a son, Jean-Paul. He'll be eighteen now and while our parents were at a conference, he was allowed to show me around Paris. You know what Frenchmen are like—romantic, gushing with compliments and very sexy...well perhaps not all Frenchman are like that, but Jean-Paul was doing his best to impress me, that's for sure. I realise now that he was just as inexperienced as I was, but the way he looked into my eyes and said..." She tried her best to imitate Jean-Paul's accent. "... *Eva, ma cherie, tu es très belle...*" She giggled and made Adele giggle too. "If any English boy had said that to me, I would have laughed in his face, but I just gazed into his dark eyes and instantly fell in love with him as we sailed down the Seine on a *Bateau Mouche*. We kissed and cuddled all the way back to his house and went to his room. Our parents were still out and we just fumbled our way through the whole thing. He was saying he loved me all the time and I just let him get on with it. In hindsight, it really wasn't romantic at all and I was too embarrassed to look at him afterwards. So all in all, complete failure. No rush of loving passion at all for either of us."

Adele looked at her best friend with sympathy. "I'm sorry, Eva. I wish you'd enjoyed it at least," and then with conviction, "I won't ever make love to anybody until I know him and love him with all my heart. I've made that promise to myself."

Eva smiled. "That's lovely, Adie," she said. "I just hope you can keep that promise. I really do."

"I shall. I know I shall."

~ * ~

The first week of the holiday flew by and both girls began to look bronzed and healthy. They chatted to the Scottish boys and Eva found herself drawn to the handsome one, Stuart, whom she had at first thought was gravitating towards Adele. Stuart and

Eva were seldom apart. Frolicking about in the pool and goodnight kisses became the foundations of a beautiful holiday romance and clearly they were both *'in the moment'* as Eva described it to her friend. Adele deliberately kept some distance between herself and the boys, but she was suddenly made aware she was being pursued by the Greek receptionist who had welcomed them when they arrived. He was tall, dark and handsome, and very charming.

"He asked me out," she told Eva. "What shall I say?"

"Say yes!" Eva exclaimed.

"But I promised Gary..."

"Adele, he hasn't asked you to marry him. Just go and have a good time," Eva urged.

His name was Cory Demetriou and he took her to a local nightspot, Club Tropicana. They had dinner whilst being entertained by Greek dancers and she laughed as the traditional smashing of plates was going on all around her. Cory was good company and the perfect gentleman. His English was almost perfect and Adele found herself bewitched by the way he described life on the island of Corfu.

"It sounds idyllic," she told him.

"Idyllic?" he asked. smiling. "That's a Greek word and it means..."

She smiled. "Perfect... Beautiful..."

"Like you," he interrupted.

Adele felt her cheeks burning and she looked down at her hands in an effort to hide her self-consciousness.

"I'm sorry, Adele," he apologised. "I did not mean to embarrass you, but I like you."

She looked up shyly. "I like you too." She heard the words come from her mouth and surprised herself that she had dared to say them, knowing she had never uttered those words to anybody, not even to Gary, her boyfriend at home.

"Shall I take you home now?" Cory suggested. "It's almost midnight and I ought not to keep you out so late."

Adele laughed. "While I'm in Corfu, I can stay up as long as I like," she told him. "No parents to come looking for me..."

"But I must do what is right," he replied. "You are sixteen; I am twenty-one...how do you say? *In loco parentis*." He smiled. "I feel responsible for you."

"Please don't say that," she pleaded. "I'm responsible enough myself to do the right thing."

"I know that," Cory continued. "I have been watching how you talk to those English boys."

"Scottish," Adele corrected.

He shrugged. "... Scottish then, but I like the way you are friends without allowing them to be...how do you say... *oikeíos* ... intimate."

Adele tapped his arm playfully. "Now you are flirting with me," she told him amicably. "I just do friendship; no need for more."

"I understand," he said. "I won't spoil it."

~ * ~

It was after their third date. They wandered along the steep pathway towards the beach. He held her hand as he helped her down the rugged steps and she thrilled at his touch. He had been the perfect gentleman, but that night there was a closeness between them that Adele had never experienced.

He drew her to him as they stepped onto the soft sand still warm from the day's sun. Their bodies came together as he gently cupped her face in his hands. Slowly, he lowered his lips to hers and they kissed passionately for the first time. "Adele; Adele," he whispered. "I have wanted to kiss you since the day I first saw you."

Adele held him close. Her heart was beating fast and she trembled at the unfamiliar feeling that coursed through her body. "I feel like I'm in another world, Cory. What is happening to me?"

He kissed her again with longing and urgency. "I love you, Adele."

Adele caught her breath. "I bet you say that to all the girls," she said in an effort to recover her equilibrium.

"No, no, I do not. I promise you, I do not," he said with more than a little assertiveness.

Adele felt the tears trickle down her cheeks. "I think I love you too, Cory. I have never felt like this and I don't want it to stop, but I leave the day after tomorrow and I will never see you again."

"If we are in love, love will find a way to keep us together," he told her gently. "Come, we will go back to the hotel to find your friends."

Adele held him back. "No, not yet," she said quietly. "Will you take me back to your quarters?"

Cory was surprised by her question. "Adele, what are you asking?" He looked directly at her. "You have no need to answer that question. I understand exactly what you are saying and you don't have to do what you are suggesting," he told her.

"I do," she said, completely unconcerned that she was abandoning all her convictions and was about to break the solemn promise she had made to herself.

~ * ~

Cory was working when the girls left the hotel on their way home. He waved and discreetly blew a kiss from behind the reception desk under the steely eye of the hotel manager. Members of staff weren't supposed to fraternise with guests so their brief relationship had been hidden during the day. Adele took a deep breath and made a concerted effort not to cry. Eva and Stuart had said their goodbyes the night before and so the two girls sat quietly, each with her own thoughts, as they wended their way to the airport, ready for the four hour flight back to England.

~ * ~

Before Adele went back to college to study history, English literature and politics, she sent a postcard to Cory with her address so that he might write back to her. The first few days at college were hectic and she began to feel very tired. She was sick when she got out of bed on a couple of mornings, but it seemed to wear off during the day. By the weekend, she became worried. She was still throwing up in the morning and her period hadn't come.

"Are you all right, Adele?" her stepmother asked. "You don't look well at all." She felt her stepdaughter's head to see if she had a fever, but it seemed to be normal.

"Don't fuss, Mum," Adele snapped. "I must have picked up a bug. I think there's been something going around at college," she lied.

"It's more likely you picked something up in that foreign country you insisted on visiting with Eva," Ivy Bartlett told her. "I don't know why you couldn't just go to Skegness like we always do. At least the water's clean."

"Stop it, Mum," Adele said wearily. "Corfu was beautiful; I didn't drink the tap water; the hotel was spotless and the food delicious. What could I possibly have picked up over there?"

"Bugs thrive in those hot climates," her stepmother continued irritatingly. "And bugs we might not be able to tolerate. They are foreign, after all."

Adele sighed deeply. "Okay, I'll go to see the doctor on Monday if I don't feel any better. Will that stop you going on about my holiday?"

Throughout her pregnancy she was completely alone. Her parents were mortified and bundled her off to St Vincent's, a home for unmarried mothers near Brighton. She sat in her room for most of the day, reading, and later being made to knit matinee jackets and baby bootees as her date of confinement came near. The stern nuns who ran the home did not allow visitors and all girls were expected to be in their own rooms by nine o'clock each night.

She had written a brief note to Eva to tell her she thought she was pregnant, but did not mention Cory. He hadn't written to her before she was sent to Brighton, but she lived in hope that her dad would forward any mail to her. Sadly, she received no reply from Eva either. In spite of this, she decided she would keep on writing, if only to unburden herself to her best friend.

Dear Eva,

I hope you don't mind my writing to you, only I don't know how you feel because you haven't answered my previous letters. You and I could always tell each other everything like when you told me your secrets in Corfu...

She stopped writing and pensively chewed on the end of her pen. Her eyes filled with tears as she thought back to her holiday in Corfu, of her promise to herself and to Eva that she would never have sex with anybody until she was sure he was the person with whom she wanted to spend the rest of her life; she thought of Cory who had been the most wonderful and gentle lover and her love for him, albeit brief and fleeting.

My baby is due in a week and I'm scared, Eva. My parents have disowned me and I am so alone, even though all the girls here are in the same boat as me. The nuns in this place are strict and I'm sure they have never heard of affection. They bark their rules and treat us as though we have committed a mortal sin just because we fell in love.

She stopped again and wiped away the hot tears as they trickled down her cheeks. Her thoughts were sad. *They all want me to give my baby away when it is born, but I refuse to do such a heartless thing. Whatever they think, I loved Cory and I believed he loved me. He seems to have disappeared from the face of the earth and I'm haunted by the thought that he has forgotten me and how wonderful we were together.*

Adele suddenly realised as she wrote that Eva might have disowned her too and may not open her letters, let alone read them.

Dearest Eva, please forgive me. I don't know what to think and I would so like to hear from you. You are my best friend and I will always love you as such. I finished with Gary as soon as I went back to college. When I came home, it was just not the same.

I don't know where I'm going to live when I leave here. My stepmother has made it clear that as long as I keep the baby, I am on my own. I live in hope that when Dad realises he has a grandchild, he, at least, will love the baby as much as I do, but I cannot count on that. My stepmother rules the roost and I am aware of the position I have put Dad in.

Please write to me, Eva. I miss you so much.

~ * ~

Aphrodite Helena Bartlett was born in the early hours of Thursday, 26 May 1960. She had dark hair and olive skin like her father and the brightest blue eyes, exactly like her mother. Her lusty cry announced to the world that she was strong and Adele smiled to herself as she thought, *My baby will survive—we will survive, whatever people might think.*

She tried to compose a letter to Cory as she had many times during the past few months, but the nagging thought that he hadn't replied to her postcard told her she knew she must accept that he had forgotten her, and what they had was, as she had convinced herself, just a holiday fling. His lack of communication since she left Corfu confirmed that.

Two weeks after Aphrodite was born, Ivy and Carlton Bartlett, Adele's parents, were allowed to visit her. Her father hugged her tightly and whispered in her ear. "Oh my goodness, Adele, what are we going to do?"

"Don't worry, Daddy. We'll be fine," she whispered back.

Her stepmother's attitude was completely different. There was no hug, no sign of affection. "Have you come to your senses and decided to give it up for adoption?" she asked brusquely.

Adele steeled herself while her stepmother continued, "There is no way we are having it in our house."

"STOP!" Adele shouted, but continued more quietly, "I hate to be rude, but stop whatever you are thinking of saying. My baby is not an 'it.' She is a girl, a beautiful little girl and I demand you recognise her as such. I will not give my baby away."

"Stupid girl," Ivy spat. "Stupid, stupid girl. How do you propose to look after her? And where are you going to live?"

Adele breathed deeply. She looked at her father who sat silently with his head bowed. Adele could see his embarrassment, but she regarded Ivy with contempt. "We'll survive," she said.

"And that's all it will be—a survival. Just think about that, Adele. We will not have you coming home with a baby. Everybody thinks you are away at college and we will not have you bringing shame on us. How could we ever show our faces at church if it were known that our daughter conceived a child out of wedlock?"

Adele gasped. "Is that all you are worried about?" she said, not hiding her feelings. "Even Mary wasn't married when…"

"Don't you dare preach at me, Adele Bartlett," her stepmother chastised. "Your child is the daughter of a Greek nobody, not conceived of the Holy Spirit…" She paused to calm herself. "How dare you liken yourself to the holy mother!"

"Oh spare me the superciliousness please," she said with disdain. "I'm not holding myself up as a paragon of virtue. You might only be my stepmother, but God forbid that you might treat me with a little motherly compassion. I have had months to think about what I have done. I am not ashamed. I loved Aphrodite's father, albeit briefly, but don't try to make me regret having my little girl, because I'll never do that."

"Aphrodite?" Ivy said scornfully. "What sort of a name is that? She'll be the laughing stock of her friends—if she has any."

"It's a beautiful name and Aphrodite is the goddess of love in Greek mythology. Her second name is Helena because that is nearest to the name of the Hotel Helenya where I stayed. She is half Greek and I love both names," Adele said almost hating herself for explaining her reasons to the unyielding woman in front of her. "Please leave if you can't accept my baby as your granddaughter." She turned to her father. "Daddy, I'm sorry you have had to witness this. I hope you will find it in your heart to accept my baby…and still love me as your daughter. I'm not asking for forgiveness, because I don't consider I need it. These things happen and I haven't suddenly become an evil person just because I got pregnant."

Ivy tutted loudly and grabbed hold of her husband's arm. "We're leaving," she snapped. "Come on, Carlton. We're done here."

Carlton Bartlett looked sadly at his beloved daughter and his expression told Adele that he had been given no choice but to go along with his wife's decision.

Adele smiled weakly at him, completely understanding his position.

Later when her tears had subsided, she found a note pushed down the side of the chair where her father had been sitting. Tentatively, she opened it and as she did so, a cheque fell out onto the floor. Without looking at the cheque she read silently.

Hello my princess. I am writing this quickly and keeping it brief. I have rarely kept secrets from Ivy, but this is one time that I know I have to act on my own. I can't pretend I'm happy with what has happened to you, but I would like you to know that I still love you and want to give you the best start for you and your baby. Your stepmother will never change her mind. She has always been stubborn and strong-willed, arrogant to a point and certainly mindful of her position within the community, especially at church. I owe her so much for the way she helped me through my grief all those years ago...and in spite of her attitude sometimes, I do love her. I have no need to explain all that to you. You understand already what she is like. Please forgive me if it seems I am abandoning you, but I know you will make more of a success with your life than if you had your stepmother breathing down your neck watching your every move.

Adele wiped away the tears that had involuntarily begun to flow again. She knew exactly that her father, who had always been nothing but loving and affectionate towards her, was basically a weak man who needed a strong woman in his life and Ivy was just that woman. It was difficult for her to believe he would find solace in a woman like her.

...Here is a cheque for £5000. It isn't our life savings, but some of the money I put away for a rainy day and Ivy knows nothing about it. I'm smiling as I acknowledge this as one of the secrets I did keep from her! I think this is the day there is torrential rain where you are and I would like you to have the money to help make the sun shine again. Put it in your bank account and before you leave St Vincent's, look in the newspaper for a place to rent until you are able to find a job. I have every faith in you.

Take care, Princess, and keep safe and well.

Your loving Dad.

~ * ~

Three months after the baby was born, mother and baby moved into a one bedroom flat on the south coast of England. Remarkably, the nuns at St Vincent's turned up trumps and provided Adele with the basic requirements to start her new life. With a single parent's allowance from the government, she determined that as soon as she was able, she would study to become a social worker. That way she might help other unsuspecting teenagers who got caught up in the bureaucratic net of unplanned pregnancy. With the money from her dad in a high interest savings account, she was able to establish herself and provide a good life for herself and Aphrodite.

Adele wrote to Eva again to inform her of the birth. Out of the blue, a reply arrived, not from Eva, but from her mother, Millicent Chesterton. It seemed Eva had received only the first letter when Adele informed her she thought she was pregnant and having told her mother of Adele's plight, Eva was instructed not to have any further contact with Adele ... *'Eva cannot be seen to have friends with no morals and so all your letters have been intercepted. Please do not contact her again.'*

Adele was both saddened and angry. *No morals?* she silently questioned. Her thoughts were harsh and very bitter and she found herself desperately searching for any shred of self-esteem to which she might cling. *What about Jean-Paul Bresson, Mrs Chesterton? At least I was over the age of consent, but you wouldn't know about Eva's fumbling with Jean-Paul, would you?* Adele sighed. She was alone and she'd have to deal with it.

Once the child was in school, Adele completed a correspondence degree course in social sciences and obtained the dream job with the local authority. Her own experience made her perfect for the role of mentor for girls who found themselves floundering in a sea of uncertainty on discovering they were pregnant. Rodi became accustomed to first one girl and then another calling her mother at odd times of the day and night. Occasionally, they allowed a girl to stay over for a few days. Since they had moved into their new house with three bedrooms, it was easy to have visitors to stay.

Adele never married. She had a few relationships, but never felt the need to permanently tie herself down to a man. Not that she was promiscuous. She had close friends, male and female, and she was happy with that. The shock of finding a lump in her breast just after her thirty-seventh birthday devastated her. She sat her twenty year old student daughter down and talked to her as gently as she could muster under such traumatic circumstances.

"You have to be strong," she said. "I'll have the treatment, but it won't be easy and nothing is guaranteed."

Rodi held on tight to her mother's hand. "Don't talk like that, Mum. Doctors can work miracles these days. We'll beat this. We've done all right so far without any help so I know we'll be all right." She took in a deep breath to prevent the sob she felt inside from surfacing.

Three months later, two days before her daughter's twenty-first birthday, Adele passed away quietly in a nursing home with Rodi by her side. Both women had been so brave and now Rodi was alone. When her mother's will was read, it heralded the beginning of a whole new life for the girl whose existence had begun in an unmarried mothers' home near Brighton in nineteen-sixty.

Two

Rodi collected her luggage and hailed a taxi to take her to the apartment she had rented.

Looking out from her balcony, she could see the old monastery as the tourists tramped up the hill to take in the views and the lifestyle of the monks who, dressed in black, seemed merely to exist as part of the tourist attraction. There was something very quaint about them; a throw-back in time and the hectic life of the nineteen-eighties seemed to have forgotten them. Rodi realised that Greece had not been forgotten. With the country joining the European Community just before she decided to make the trip, Greece had enabled her to take a long working holiday until she found her father. The task ahead of her was enormous.

~ * ~

"How long are you going to be away, Rodi?" Matthew asked when he called.

"Please, Matthew, not again. I don't know how long it will take. I have no idea where to start looking at the moment," she said as gently as she was able.

"What about me, Rodi?" he asked. "I'm your boyfriend, the person you have left behind. Can't you at least give me an idea when I might see you again? The thought of you being in Greece all on your own scares me." He stopped abruptly before he said what he was thinking: *Look what happened to your mum.*

Rodi sighed. "I thought we'd gone over all this," she said. "Please don't make this any more difficult than it is already."

Matthew sighed too. "I'm not trying to make it difficult, Rodi. I'm just facing facts."

"What facts?" Rodi snapped. "The fact that I lost my mother whose dying wish was that I should find my father? The fact that the task before me is more than I can possibly imagine at the moment? The fact that I need to find the man who left my mother in the lurch?" She breathed in deeply. "Or is it the fact that you have both parents alive and well and don't have to go searching to find out who you are?"

"That's a little below the belt, Rodi," Matthew told her, not trying to hide his disappointment in her.

Rodi felt a lump rise in her throat. "Sorry," she croaked. "I have so much on my plate at the moment and I have no idea where to start. I think I'm going to get a job as soon as possible. I'll need to fund my stay."

Matthew was heartened by her positive thinking albeit very superficial at this point. "I have a suggestion," he said cheerily. "Why don't you try waitressing at the hotel where your mum and her friend stayed? They might have records, you know, maybe forwarding addresses of past employees." His tone was encouraging, his thoughts less so. *The sooner she gets this damned business over, the better.*

Rodi was heartened by his positivity. "Good idea, although I've never been a waitress," she told him. "Maybe I'll just go and see what jobs are available. The holiday season begins in a few weeks and with my qualifications, I might be able to do something as an entertainment, or children's rep. I feel better already. Thanks, Matty. I owe you one."

"Just come home safe and sound to me when all this is over, babe," he said with feeling. "I want my Rodi back, with or without a father."

"I know," she replied, trying not to sound placatory, "and knowing that you are waiting for me is all the support I need."

Matthew sighed again. "Good luck, Rodi. I think you'll need it." With that he was gone.

~ * ~

"When are you able to start work?" the entertainments rep asked her.

Rodi grinned. "Now..." she said with a twinkle in her eye.

"Ha ha, very funny," he replied sarcastically.

"I'm serious," she said, not quite able to believe her luck. "I am available right now if you need me. I'd like to learn the ropes before the season starts."

The rep looked at her wide-eyed. "I have never interviewed anybody so enthusiastic," he told her. "I'm impressed and here you are with a primary teaching qualification. I can't believe my luck in finding such a suitable children's rep for the summer season. I'm Jake, by the way and you'll be answerable to me at all times." He grinned at her amicably. "Just make sure you don't make any mistakes or I'll be down on you like a tonne of bricks."

"Yes sir, Jake sir!" she answered jokingly. "When can I start then?"

Jake looked her in the eye. "Come in tomorrow at nine o'clock and we'll make a start on the children's programme. I can tell you about the general procedure while we're at it. As a teacher, you'll know how to deal with children and from what I've seen so far, the kids will love you. There'll be four of you in your team. I'd like to make you team leader as the others are younger than you and have already been selected by the travel company. We'll be employed directly by the hotel and will incorporate the others into our programme. Hotel Helenya and Grecian Tours work closely together."

The following morning, she donned her new uniform of white shorts and yellow, blue and white striped blouse and arrived ten minutes early so as to show her eagerness to start work. Jake was behind the reception desk when she arrived and he waved across the foyer as she appeared at the top of the marble steps.

"Hi Rodi...that's some name, by the way!" he called. "Come and meet some of the hotel staff."

~ * ~

The holiday season began slowly at first. The hotel wasn't full during May, but come June, July and August, there was no time to breathe. When Rodi wasn't occupied with the children, she was planning new activities and rehearsing for the weekly concert. Tourists loved the acts performed by the reps, and the reps in turn delighted in making fools of themselves for a couple of hours. Rodi discovered she could sing, or more to the point that she enjoyed singing for an audience. She was given ballads to sing which nearly always brought a tear to the eye of unsuspecting holiday-makers.

"How come a song as old as 'Danny Boy' makes people cry?" she asked.

Jake smiled. "I don't know, but even my dad sheds a tear when he hears that well-loved song. I think it's called 'Londonderry Air' really." He nudged her playfully. "Mind you, with a name like Patrick, I'm not surprised he gets emotional when he hears it. He left Ireland when he was a teenager, but he still calls Ireland home."

Rodi smiled back at him. Her curiosity was heightened by this snippet of information and she wondered if Jake's father kept in touch with home. Until then, she had kept her real reason for being in Corfu under wraps. "Does he ever try to find his old friends?" she asked.

"Sometimes, but such a lot of them emigrated so it's difficult to know where they are," Jake told her. "Why do you ask? Have you got friends in Ireland?"

Rodi sighed. She wasn't sure she ought to be divulging too much information at this point. "Well..." she offered, "I am trying to find somebody—not in Ireland, but I really don't have any idea where to start."

"What's wrong, Rodi?" Jake asked as he detected a glazed look in her previously shining eyes.

"Nothing wrong," she said.

Jake gently took her hand. "It doesn't take a super brain to work out that you are here for something other than a holiday job. A person as well qualified as you does not just appear out of the blue and ask for a job in a hotel. Are you running away from something?"

Rodi sprung to her own defence. "No, of course not, but I do have a reason for being here in Paleocastritsa. My mother holidayed here in nineteen fifty-nine."

"A long time ago," Jake stated matter-of-factly. "It's probably changed beyond recognition. For instance, the west wing was only constructed last year after a fire totally wiped out the reception area. All records of staff and visitors were lost. That's why we are starting from scratch this season—new organisation, new staff, new everything."

"Oh no!" Rodi exclaimed with feeling.

"Why? What's wrong?" Jake asked curiously.

Rodi felt her heart was breaking and tears welled up in her eyes. "Oh Jake," she cried. "This makes my task impossible."

Jake continued to hold her hand gently to reassure her that she wasn't alone. "Tell me what's bothering you, Rodi, and I might be able to help."

Still holding her hand in his, Jake listened attentively as Rodi related the story of her mother, Adele Bartlett and of Cory Demetriou. "She never told me his name until she died and it's so frustrating that I can no longer ask her the questions to which I need answers," she explained. "I'm really not sure who she was protecting—me, or herself. Her parents had nothing to do with her after I was born. I only met my grandfather once after his wife had passed away. I was only four at the time and about a year afterwards, he was killed in a road accident so Mum and I were completely alone."

"That's so sad," Jake sympathised.

"Oh please don't feel sorry for us," she pleaded. "We had a very good life and Mum's inheritance made us reasonably well-off. My grandfather had provided for her in his will even though he hadn't been part of her life for a long time. Mum was always philosophical about her life in general." She felt comfortable sharing this information with Jake. Somehow, she felt a close affiliation to him.

"We'll get the season over with and then we'll start looking," Jake told her. "If you are in agreement, I'll make arrangements for us to be kept here for the closed season so we will be able to scour Greece from top to bottom if needs be. Okay?"

Rodi looked directly at him. "You don't have to do that," she told him firmly. "What will your family think? Your wife? Partner? Anybody who is close to you?"

He patted her knee affectionately. "My family are in England, that is, my mum and dad and my brother and his family. I have no wife—well, not anymore and I have no immediate intentions of taking up with anybody else while I'm here working all hours God sends. I'll enjoy helping you...that is, if you would like me to."

"I'd appreciate all the help I can get. Thanks, Jake. You're a mate!"

Jake smiled at her and thought he liked the girl he had only recently met. *Like?* he asked himself silently, but he refused to allow his thoughts to run away with him.

Three

Once the season was in full swing, Rodi delighted in the vast numbers of British people who chose to holiday in Corfu. The children loved her and hung on to her hand whenever possible as they eagerly went about the exciting activities arranged for them.

"Rodi?" Jennifer asked in the middle of a face-painting session.

"Yes," Rodi replied as she continued to paint leopard spots and whiskers on Jennifer's little brother's face.

"Why have you got such a funny name?" the girl asked innocently.

"Rodi smiled. "I don't think it's funny," she said rather more defensively than she would have liked.

The child continued unabashed. "Well, not funny, but different."

Rodi chose not to furnish this inquisitive eleven-year-old with details. "My mum liked it and as you say, it is different. Why are you called Jennifer?"

"I guess because my mum liked that name too," the girl replied just as her mother approached.

"Is Jenny annoying you?" the lady asked. "She can be quite a chatterbox given a good listener. Please feel free to tell her to be quiet."

"It's all right," Rodi told her, smiling amicably. "It's all part and parcel of the job."

The lady looked wide-eyed. "You sound very like me," she observed. "Where do you come from?"

"I was born in Brighton, but I have lived in Worthing for most of my life," Rodi explained.

"Well, that doesn't place me near you at all," the woman said. "So much for my ability in detecting accents. I come from Grantham in Lincolnshire although we live in London now."

Rodi smiled. "Well, my mum came from near there so maybe I've picked up a bit of her accent along the way."

"At least it gives me a little bit of credibility. Thanks for that... Oh, I don't know your name, sorry."

"Well, that's what your daughter found intriguing," Rodi told her. "My name is spelt R-O-D-I—pronounced *roady,* and short for Aphrodite. I always have to explain it."

"Well, yes, it is unusual, but I can understand why you are in Greece with a name like that and in this place in particular. I love it here. My husband and I have come back every couple of years since we were married. This hotel holds a special place in my heart."

"I've never been here, but I'm growing to love it too," Rodi said.

"Oh you will probably fall madly in love with Corfu in general, but this place is special," the woman continued. "What time do you finish? I hope you will come and join us for drinks after dinner…if you can. We can talk about Corfu and the home country then if you like."

"That would be lovely," Rodi said. "I finish at seven tonight. I'll see you in the lounge bar about nine. Is that all right?"

"Perfect. Oh and by the way, I'm Eva and my husband is Jean-Paul."

~ * ~

At nine o'clock precisely, Rodi made her way to the lounge bar to meet Eva and Jean-Paul. She had changed from her uniform and dressed in a pale turquoise sun-dress, her tanned skin and dark hair shining in the soft lights of the bar. Her blue eyes, inherited from her mother, were sparkling and Eva audibly gasped when she saw her.

"Hello again, Rodi," she called as Rodi approached. "This is my husband, Jean-Paul Bresson."

Jean-Paul stood up and offered his hand. "I am pleased to meet you, Rodi," he said with the smallest trace of a French accent which Rodi loved.

"Hello," Rodi said. "How are you?"

"I'm well, very well, thank you," he replied. "Do sit down and what would you like to drink?"

"Just a soft drink, thank you. Fanta lemon, please. I must keep a clear head. Keeping children occupied in this heat does not call for dealing with a hangover at the same time," she said light-heartedly.

"Indeed not," Eva chipped in and then added, "We really appreciate what you do for the children. You and your colleagues make our holiday much more enjoyable knowing that our children are in safe hands."

Rodi smiled amicably. "All in a day's work," she said.

The conversation was light and Rodi found the information about Corfu interesting. "I haven't had time to travel around the island yet, but I intend to do just that at the end of the season and possibly go over to the mainland too. Jake is going to travel with me." She felt she ought to stop before she disclosed her real reason for travelling around Greece.

Eva looked at Rodi with raised eyebrows. "Are you two…?"

"Oh no!" Rodi interrupted vehemently. "I want to see Greece; he's offered to show me. As simple as that."

"Don't your parents want you home at the end of the season?" Jean-Paul asked.

Rodi sighed. "My mother passed away last year…"

"Oh, I'm sorry." He looked across at his wife. "We both are."

Eva nodded in agreement. "Perhaps we should talk about happier things," she said. "Tell me, have you always wanted to be a children's rep in a holiday hotel?"

Rodi smiled. "Not really," she admitted. "I'm a trained primary school teacher. I finished my training just before I came out here. It was either going to Barrowton where my mother was brought up, or coming out to Corfu. A no brainer really, so here I am."

Eva sat up straight in her chair. "Barrowton?" she asked in wonder. "I only knew one person from Barrowton. What are the odds of it being your mum?"

"Yes, that's where my mum was born. She went to school in Grantham so maybe you knew her," Rodi suggested. "I guess that's the link in our accents."

Eva's heart began to beat wildly in her chest. She took a deep breath to steady herself and Jean-Paul noticed.

"What is it, *ma cherie*?" he asked as he took her hand as a sign of support for whatever it was that had made his wife go pale. "Are you feeling unwell?"

Eva swallowed and shook her head slowly as she asked quietly, "What was her name? Perhaps I might have heard of her."

Rodi was confused by Eva's reaction. "She was called Adele Bartlett..."

Eva's gasp could not be hidden. "Oh my goodness," she whispered and she could not prevent the tears from trickling down her cheeks. "Oh my goodness," she said again. "You have no idea how sad I am to hear of her death. Dear, dear Adele. I let her down so badly..."

Rodi did not know how to react. "Are you saying you actually knew Mum?" she asked in amazement. "This is ridiculous. She never talked about you; she never talked freely about anybody from her past. There was always something too painful about it so I never knew about her friends other than the ones we both knew. Her philosophy on life was that you live for the present; forget the past and look forward to the future. Did you really know her?" She stopped and breathed deeply in order to take in what she had just heard.

Eva sobbed and nodded as she wiped away her tears. "Adele was my dearest friend," she admitted now. "We came here on our first holiday without parents when we were sixteen." She related how they had enjoyed their two weeks in the sun and then Adele had written to say that she had discovered she was pregnant. When I told my mum, she was furious and forbade me to see Adele again. Teenage pregnancies in those days were absolutely taboo, especially for girls who went to Ousthwaite's College for Young Ladies.

"Then the next I knew, Adele had gone away and I never heard from her again. I never knew what had happened to her and I assumed she didn't want to keep in touch with me." She looked pleadingly at Rodi. "Please forgive me, Rodi, but I was so shocked when she said she was pregnant. She had always vowed she would never have sex until she found her Mister Right. I just presumed that she had arrived home and slept with her boyfriend and that surprised me. She never told me who the father of her child was."

Rodi's eyes filled with hot tears as she observed the desperation in Eva's face. "Please don't feel guilty," she said gently. "Mum always told me that she loved my father, albeit briefly."

"Was Gary your father? He was the boy she was staying faithful to while she was here in Paleocastritsa."

Now it was Rodi's turn to be sad. "No, I've never heard of anybody called Gary. Mum was a single mother right up until her death. It was only when her will was read that I finally found out my father's name is Cory Demetriou."

Eva gasped again. "Oh my goodness!" she exclaimed. "I never knew she had given herself to Cory. She kept that secret from me. Maybe she thought she had let me down after her promise. Oh, Rodi, I don't know what to say."

Rodi's heart was beating madly. "Did you know Cory?" she asked excitedly. "Did you know my father? Have you seen him since that holiday in nineteen fifty-nine? Do you know where he is? Can you…"

"Whoa there, sweetheart," Eva said to the excited Rodi. "I haven't seen, nor heard of him since that holiday. I just know he liked your mum as soon as he set eyes on her, and she resisted his invitations at first, but I encouraged her to have a little fling while we were on holiday. I couldn't see any harm in an innocent holiday romance, but oh my word. How could I have ever known what might happen? Adele was the most intelligent, caring, sincere and understanding person I knew. I trusted her with my deepest secrets—indeed, I divulged my innermost secret to her on that holiday." She looked lovingly at her husband. "Remember the *Bateau Mouche*, darling?"

Jean-Paul grinned and nodded knowingly.

"Well, I told Adele about that and what happened afterwards," she continued. "As I said, I could trust her with my life."

"But if you came back here after you were married, was Cory Demetriou still here?" Rodi asked, hoping against hope that Eva had seen him.

Eva took hold of Rodi's hand. "Oh, sweetheart, Jean-Paul and I didn't marry until nineteen sixty-nine, ten years after that holiday. We both went to university and didn't get together until after we had finished our courses. Hence, our first child, Jennifer, is only now eleven years old. We were late starters in the parent stakes. By then all the staff here had changed. Have you asked at reception if they know where he is?"

Rodi explained about the fire.

"I did know about that, but I didn't even think about staff records," Eva said. "I wish I could help, but I can't. I was just a girl when I came with Adele." Her eyes filled with tears again. "I do wish I'd known where she had gone. I would certainly have been there to support her, but my mother strictly forbade me to see her. I feel so guilty that I didn't try harder."

"It's not your fault and I'm not sure you could have done anything different. Her own parents disowned her—well, her stepmother did, but her dad made sure she was financially taken care of."

Eva sighed deeply. "That I can well understand. Her stepmother always had grandiose ideas and I don't think I'm speaking out of turn in saying that. Adele was very close to her dad, but I guess he had to keep his wife happy. Are they still alive?"

Rodi shook her head and explained the circumstances of their deaths.

"How sad," Jean-Paul said, having allowed Eva and Rodi to explore the past without interruption.

"Please don't be sad for us. We were very happy and anyway, Mum got a social science degree and became a counsellor for unmarried mothers. She loved her job and she was perfectly suited to it."

"That's the Adele I knew and loved," Eva beamed. "She was the most genuine person I ever met. I'm so pleased she was happy."

By the end of the evening, they had gleaned lots of interesting information from each other and after the initial shock of discovering each other's identity, they parted with smiles on their faces.

"We leave tomorrow," Eva told her, "but please keep in touch. I feel so close to Adele again through you, Rodi." She smiled affectionately at the thought of Rodi's name. "Adele knew what she was doing when she gave you your name, didn't she?"

"She certainly did," Rodi agreed. "I'm Aphrodite Helena and I think you'll have guessed by now that my real reason for being here is to find my father. That was Mum's final request. I have to do it; I just have to."

Unknown to the party sitting in the lounge bar that fateful evening, the young barman had pricked up his ears on hearing the name Cory Demetriou. His English wasn't good and so the gist of the conversation was lost on him, but he smiled to himself. Stavros Roussos considered what he might do. Silently he plotted and schemed. *Cory Demetriou, eh?*

Four

The holiday season finished officially at the end of October. With all of the guests gone, the entertainment staff stayed on to clear up and formulate plans for next season. Rodi and Jake looked forward to the challenge that had the potential of becoming a real life-changing experience for Rodi at least.

"Let's go to the police first and see if they can tell me where to start," Rodi suggested. "There might be some sort of records office we can check out."

Jake looked into the bright eyes of the girl he had grown to adore during the past few months. "Let me talk to a few of the staff first," he said. "Somebody might know Cory Demetriou, or his family at least."

Rodi was uncertain and it showed in her eyes. "I don't want to be the talk of the staff," she said.

"I'll be discreet; I promise," Jake told her.

"Okay, but please don't mention my name."

~ * ~

"My parents met him around nineteen fifty-nine," Jake told the hotel manager. "Were you here then?"

The manager eyed him curiously. "How come you are only just asking about him? You've been here a couple of years. Why now?"

Jake thought quickly. "My mother was going through some old photos and this Demetriou chap was in the background on a couple of them," he explained. "A handsome bloke, according to my mum."

"Fancied him, did she?" the manager smirked. "I see holiday flings all the time."

"I don't know," Jake said as he joined in the little charade. "I was just a toddler at the time so if she did, I wouldn't have noticed, but I don't think my dad would have allowed her to flirt with anybody. They were so in love—still are." Tiring of the dramatization, he asked, "Well, do you know him or not?"

The manager shrugged and turned to walk away. "I've never heard of him," he said and laughed loudly. "Why is it so important anyway? I can't see the point of looking for somebody you don't know, and so long ago too." Then he was gone.

Jake sighed. The manager was his last resort and he'd been just about as useful as a wheel-less car. He dug his hands deep in his pockets and set off to find Rodi to tell her the sad news, but his spirits were lifted as he passed the bar.

"Hey, Jake," Roussos, the barman called. "You want Cory Demetriou? I know about him..."

Jake stopped in his tracks.

Stavros Roussos continued. "I hear the English girl, Rodi, talking about him too. I not understand, but she keep saying his name."

Jake instinctively grabbed the barman's arms and gripped tightly as he asked, "What do you know?" He released his grip in order not to appear aggressive, but he didn't like this guy and he realised immediately that this person whom he did not trust had brought Rodi into the equation when she expressly asked not to be mentioned.

"I know she get...how you say...excited when she say his name. She want him bad."

Jake looked into Roussoss's eyes. They were cold and furtive. "Please tell me what you know," he said in an effort not to make too much of a deal of the situation and thinking, *After all, it is an innocent search and I consider that antagonising this man might give the wrong impression, but I need him to tell me what he knows.* "I would like to meet up with Cory Demetriou if we can find him." And then as an afterthought, "My mother would like to contact him again. They used to be friends. She has some souvenirs for him from long ago."

Roussos eyed him closely. "What for me?" he asked in broken English. "How I know you not bad for him? And why the Rodi girl asking about him before you?"

Jake began to feel uncomfortable. He didn't like the man, so had never made a friend of him as he had with the other hotel employees. Roussos was a stranger, a loner, always smouldering, always having a shifty look about him. "Are you asking me for money?" he questioned.

Roussos shrugged. "Please yourself then," he snapped. "You pay; I tell."

Jake shrugged now. "No way," he said firmly. "You're making this sound like I'm asking for something illegal. All I want to do is trace a long lost friend." He turned and walked away leaving Roussos to stew on the fact that his stupid little extortion plan had failed.

Rodi was beside herself. "What if he really did know something, Jake?" she wailed. "Couldn't I just leave the money anonymously in exchange for the information?"

"No!" Jake told her sharply. "It's sordid; he's sordid. I wouldn't trust him as far as I could throw him. There must be another way to help us find a clue as to Demetriou's whereabouts."

"Let's try the old guy who does the gardens," Rodi suggested. "He's old enough to have been here a long time. It's worth a try."

Jake looked pensive. "I think I'd like to try the police first. I'm not sure how trustworthy these locals are. Many of them say very little, but they don't miss much. Look at that snake Roussos. He had been listening in to your conversation with the Bressons and he remembered even though it was weeks ago. Please, Rodi. Try the police first. The fewer people round here who know what we're doing, the better. It's none of their business and we don't want to invite speculation, especially if Demetriou has dealings with Roussos. The mind boggles at the thought."

"But doesn't it make me seem as shifty as Roussos if I'm not open about it?" Rodi asked.

Jake took hold of her hand and looked into her eyes. His thoughts belied the calmness he was displaying as he spoke. *God, I love this girl, but there's the problem of her boyfriend in England. Don't go there, Jake.* "There is something about Roussos that disturbs me, Rodi. I think he might know something, but the mere fact he's asked for money makes it seem dodgy. And how do we know that Cory Demetriou is reliable?"

Rodi gasped. "I know because he's my father and my mother wouldn't ..." She stopped as she realised that perhaps her father wasn't as reliable as she had thought. After all, he had allowed her mother... "I hate to think of it, but maybe you're right, Jake. He didn't even try to contact my mother after she left Corfu." She shivered involuntarily. "Maybe he had a different girl every week. The turnover of guests is very regular." She sighed and tears welled up in her eyes.

Jake pulled her into his arms and hugged her tightly. "Don't cry, darling. We'll find him even if we have to spend the rest of our lives searching." His heart was beating wildly in his chest, but Rodi didn't seem to notice.

~ * ~

After two long and hot hours in the local police office, Rodi and Jake were given little hope.

"The man has no police record so we do not have any information of his whereabouts," the kindly officer told them. "You have to understand that our records only go back as far as the year this office opened in nineteen seventy-four, an important year for Greece."

"Where would you suggest we start looking?" Rodi asked. "Are there any census records?"

"Of course, but there are only limited resources here in Corfu," the officer said. "You will have to go to Athens."

Rodi's face dropped, but Jake was there to support her. "That's fine," he said. "Thanks for your help."

Once outside, Rodi grabbed Jake's hand. "Athens?" she asked wide-eyed.

Jake grinned. "Exciting, isn't it?"

Rodi relaxed. "Well, yes it is," she agreed. "I would love to go to Athens, but will there be the information we require when we get there?"

Jake shrugged. "Who knows? But it's a start." He kissed her on the forehead.

Rodi stood stock still. She was still holding Jake's hand and as she looked into his eyes, she saw what she didn't expect at all, but she shivered involuntarily at the thrill.

Jake smiled. "Come on, let's get back. We'll try the Corfu records first. It's worth a try. If that fails, we'll fly to Athens at the weekend." The young couple walked back to the hotel hand in hand, Jake with a very contented smile on his face, Rodi happy to go along with it.

~ * ~

There was a stunned silence at the other end of the line. Rodi waited with bated breath. When she broke the silence, she asked quietly. "Well? Are you going to say anything?"

There was another pregnant pause and then Matthew began. "Well, it's a good job I didn't stay faithful to you all summer then, isn't it?"

Rodi gasped. "I *haven't* been unfaithful to you," she said forcefully. "It's just that I don't know when I'll be back, and if I renew my contract at the hotel for next year, it's going to be a long time before I see you again. I think I'm doing the right thing in finishing with you for now. It will give you time to play the field..." She paused significantly. "...Oh, but it seems you've already started doing that, haven't you? And I thought I could trust you. Ah well, it's only fair to have told you, then you don't have to do it behind my back anymore." Her tone wasn't antagonistic.

"Don't play the innocent with me, Rodi," Matthew said. He didn't hide the scorn in his voice. "I knew what would happen when you left so I didn't sit licking my wounds, if that's what you think. Like mother, like daughter, eh?"

"What are you saying, Matt?" she cried. "That's an awful thing to say and your attitude doesn't become you at all. I thought I knew you, but perhaps I didn't know you well enough."

"Not my fault, Rodi," he replied, still trying to keep the upper hand. "No guy would sit around all summer waiting for his supposed girlfriend to go gadding around Greece on a wild goose chase. I'm sorry if you're shocked at my attitude, but it's you who is delivering the final blow."

"That's true and I'm sorry," Rodi said as she thought, *I actually feel relieved to be ending it with Matt*. "I have too much going on in my life just now to think about keeping a long distance relationship going. Please will you try to understand?"

"Oh I understand all right," Matthew said with more than a hint of sarcasm in his tone. "Jake, is it?"

"No!"

"Whatever you say, Rodi, whatever you say. I hope for your sake he delivers everything he's promising, because from what you have told me, he's keener than you think. Work it out for yourself, Rodi." With that he was gone.

Five

"He would have been born in nineteen thirty-eight, or thereabout," Rodi told the librarian who was a taciturn man and appeared to be in his late fifties. She could hardly contain the thrill of starting the search in earnest.

The librarian looked at Jake and spoke to him. "Please, lady. Don't get excited," he instructed. "I will see what I can find." With that he disappeared through a door behind the desk and left Rodi and Jake standing there quite dumbfounded by the librarian's demeanour. In about ten minutes he returned with two enormous volumes and ushered the young people to a desk in the main body of the library building. "Look through these," he said and left them to browse the gigantic tomes he had brought for them.

Trying to find their way around the Greek list of births for nineteen thirty-eight was like walking blindfolded through a forest. The Greek alphabet was their biggest obstacle and the sour-faced librarian didn't seem to be interested. On the next desk was a young student who picked up on their plight.

"Can I help?" she asked.

Rodi breathed a sigh of relief. "Yes please," she said and she explained what they were looking for.

The girl scanned the pages looking for the name Demetriou... *Demis, Alexander, Alexei, Nikolas, Dion*... "Such a lot of Demetrious in Corfu," she said. *Dion, Kristoff, Colin.* She ran her finger down the list. *Petros*... She paused. "Petros, father, mother Eleni, children Ariadnê and Cory..."

Rodi gasped and grabbed hold of the girl's arm. "Show me, please," she said excitedly.

The girl pointed out the names and lingered with her finger on the name of the son, *Cory. "Born 26 May 1938 in Lakones."*

"Where is Lakones? Is there an address?" Rodi asked, hardly able to contain herself.

"It is not too far away. North side of Paleokastritsa, but no address."

"Quite a few of the staff come from there. It's only a small village," Jake told her. He saw how Rodi's eyes were shining with tears about to trickle down her cheeks. He considered he needed to get her out of the library and work out their next move. "Thank you so much," he said to the young girl. "We really appreciate what you have done. Thank you." He took hold of Rodi's hand and guided her through the door into the narrow streets of Corfu Town.

Once outside, Rodi allowed the tears to flow. "Oh Jake, do you think we have found him already?" she asked, "And he even has the same birthday I have. That can't be coincidence, can it? It has to be him."

"Hold on, Rodi," Jake said gently. "We can't be sure about anything. Don't build up your hopes. If he's not there, you will be so disappointed."

Back in Rodi's apartment, they made their plans. "It's too late to go to Lakones tonight," Jake said. "We can't go knocking on people's doors in the dark. Let's get up early in the morning and go soon after breakfast. I'll pick you up about nine-thirty."

"You can sleep on my settee if you like," Rodi suggested, "Then we can really have an early start."

Jake's heart leapt in his chest. "Thanks, but no thanks, Rodi. I'd rather sleep in my bed. I've done settees before and they are not comfortable."

"Okay, but don't be late!" she said with a grin.

"I wouldn't dare," he replied with a wink at the girl who was stealing his heart and, kissing her affectionately on the cheek, he whispered, "Goodnight. See you tomorrow."

~ * ~

Jake arrived on the dot of nine-thirty. "Hi," he greeted his friend. "Did you sleep well?"

Rodi shook her head. "Not well at all," she told him. "I kept going over and over what has happened, trying to think what I would say to my dad when I meet him, but I came up with very little."

"Don't try to plan anything, Rodi," Jake advised. "It never works out as you plan."

"I know that, but..." She paused poignantly. "How do you inform a guy you are his daughter when he is totally unaware of your existence?"

Jake took her hand. "Don't stress, babe. We haven't found him yet and you have to be prepared for not finding him today, or next week..." He paused knowing he had to emphasise what he was going to say next. "Let's face it, we may never find him."

"Please don't say that, Jake," Rodi cried. "I have to find him. He's a comparatively young man, only in his forties, so it would have to be a very cruel twist of fate for him to have died young like my mum. No, somehow I know he is alive and well...and I'll find him if it's the last thing I do."

Jake's little Fiat car chugged along the dusty road to Lakones. Rodi sat quietly, her heart beating wildly in her chest. As Jake pulled up outside the local general store, she asked, "Where do we start?"

"Right here," Jake replied.

"At the store?"

"Exactly," he continued. "Everybody in the village will use the store. We ought to be able to get some information from the storekeeper."

"Good idea, Jake," Rodi said with a smile. "I do appreciate your being here. I need somebody who can view this whole situation through unemotional eyes."

"Hold on, Miss Bartlett," Jake interrupted. "I'm almost as emotionally involved as you are. I don't think you realise how you transmit everything you feel to me." He stopped short of telling her he loved her. "I'm your friend and I care about this."

Rodi looked at him with affection. "Thanks, Jake. I don't know how I will ever repay your kindness."

"We'll find a way, I'm sure, when all this is over."

The storekeeper was a round, balding man with a welcoming smile. "*Kaliméra*," he said.

"Good morning. Do you speak English?" Jake asked.

"A little."

"Perhaps you can help us," Jake continued and then looked guiltily at Rodi. "Do you want to ask, or shall I?"

Rodi signalled to him to carry on.

The storekeeper looked curious.

"We are trying to find a friend from long ago," Jake informed him. "He came from Lakones and his name is Cory Demetriou.

We know he lived here in nineteen fifty-nine, but we don't know where he went after that."

The storekeeper appeared to be uncomfortable with the enquiry and he shook his head slowly. "I don't know this man, but I do not like you asking me for information. You put me in a—how do you say—*adéxios*..."

Jake's understanding of Greek was limited, but some of the hotel's clients had been described as *'adéxios'* on numerous occasions. "Awkward," he translated.

"Yes, awkward," the storekeeper said. "If I know the guy, but I do not, he not want me give you information." His English was very stilted.

"We understand," Jake told him in an effort to reassure him. "We are asking for a very genuine reason. Is there anybody in the village by the name of Demetriou?"

The storekeeper shook his head. "I live here only five years. The oldest man in Lakones is Yannis Papakostas. He usually come later. I ask him. You come back at twelve o'clock."

Rodi sighed. "Please, can you tell us where he lives? We really need to talk to him."

The storekeeper looked uncomfortable again. "I not think I can. Sorry."

Jake realised the dilemma. "Don't worry about it."

"Sorry," the storekeeper said again as they left.

Rodi was disheartened and it showed in her whole demeanour, but Jake peered into her eyes and said gently. "Rodi, this is just the beginning. We've had a little setback, but it's not the end of the world. The guy didn't know Cory Demetriou. He has only lived here for five years. How could he if Cory Demetrious moved on years ago? We'll ask the next person we see if he—she—knows where Yannis Papakostas lives. We might get lucky."

They sat in the car for a short while and then set off slowly heading north to the edge of the village. Jake laughed out loud.

"What are you laughing at?" Rodi asked.

"We are going so slow, it looks like we're kerb-crawling," Jake explained. "There's a law against that in the UK. I hope there isn't a strong police presence in Lakones."

Rodi laughed too. "Well, I don't think this person looks like a lady of the night," she said as she pointed out a tiny woman dressed in black from head to toe sitting by her front door.

"No, but she might know the Demetriou family. Let's stop and ask."

Rodi quickly wound her window down to the bottom and smiled at the lady who nodded and returned a half-smile to her. "Do you speak English?" she asked.

The lady grimaced. "*Ty?*"

"English?" Rodi repeated.

The lady shook her head, but called out. "*Alec? Boreí na sas voithísei parakaló?*" Alec, can you help me, please?

Alec, a young man of about eighteen, appeared at the door. Looking at the car that had stopped outside the house, he asked, "*Ti symvaínei, yiayia?*" What's up, Nana?

Rodi asked the young man, "Do you speak English?"

"I do," Alec replied. "How can I help?"

Rodi decided to choose her words carefully in order not to get the point blank refusal they had received from the storekeeper. "We are trying to find an old friend who used to live in Lakones many years ago. He was a friend of my mother's and she passed away last year. We have been told that Yannis Papakostas might know where he is," she explained. "Can you direct us to where Mr Papakostas lives, please?"

At the sound of the name Yannis Papakostas, the lady who, on observation, didn't look as old as they had first imagined, caught hold of her grandson's arm. She communicated in Greek that the said man had gone to Thessaloniki to be with his daughter. Alec translated.

Rodi immediately became disheartened again and Jake got out of the car to talk to the young man himself. "We are trying to locate a gentleman by the name of Cory Demetriou. Does he, or his family still live in Lakones?"

Alec shrugged, but asked his grandmother if she knew anybody by the name of Demetriou.

She looked pensive, but answered for her grandson to interpret. "Many years ago there was a young family called Demetriou in Lakones. The father was a chef at Hotel Helenya."

"That's him!" Rodi interrupted excitedly. "It surely must be Cory's father. That's why he was working at the hotel when Mum met him."

"Rodi," Jake said in an effort to calm her down. "Give them a chance without interrupting—please."

The lady continued. "There was a tragedy, a very sad situation. The mother and her daughter left the house one night while the father was at work. They took all their belongings and just left without saying where they were going."

"Oh my goodness," Rodi cried. "What happened to the son?"

"The son lived in quarters at the hotel where he worked, I believe, but when the father came home and found his wife had left, he got very drunk. He walked around Lakones shouting for his wife and because it was dark—you will have noticed there are no street lights here in Lakones—a car came speeding round the corner and hit him. He was killed outright."

"Oh my goodness," Rodi said again and felt tears involuntarily trickle down her cheeks. "That's so sad," she said. "So very, very sad."

Jake tried to keep a calm outlook for Rodi's sake. "Did the son attend the funeral?"

The old lady wasn't sure. "There were rumours that there had been problems in the marriage for a long time and I don't know anything about the son. He had left home. Nobody has seen any of them since then."

Jake was curious. "Are you able to put a date to this?"

"Not really," the lady said. "Most of what I'm telling you is what I've been told myself. As you can imagine, it was the talk of the village for a long time. I was working in Athens when it happened. It must have been sometime between nineteen fifty-eight and nineteen seventy. I can't say exactly."

Rodi took the lady's hand and thanked her. The lady smiled and squeezed Rodi's hand. "I understand how you feel about your mama. I lost my husband last year." She fingered the fabric of her skirt and waved it around slightly to indicate the reason for her black clothes.

With that, Rodi felt an unexplainable closeness to her and instinctively gave her a hug. "Thank you, Nana," she whispered. "Thank you."

Six

Back in Rodi's apartment, she flopped onto the sofa, her whole demeanour one of complete dejection. "One step forward; ten steps back," she declared. "We are back at square one."

"Don't get all despondent on me again, Rodi," Jake said. "I thought we made progress today. We know the family lived in Lakones. We learned there were things happening in Cory's life that might have prevented him from contacting your mum. That has to be a bit more reassuring as regards his character. To my mind, that can only be a positive...much better than the thought of his being a friend of Stavros Roussos."

Rodi sighed. "I still haven't ruled out that Roussos might know something," she said thoughtfully. "What if I ask him myself? He might not ask me for money like he did you."

Jake gasped. "You are kidding me, aren't you?"

"No, I'm not. I'll take any information that's on offer at the moment. What if he knows where the family went?" Rodi was clutching at straws. "Jake, please don't pour cold water on everything I suggest," she said plaintively.

Jake breathed in deeply and went to sit beside her on the sofa. Taking her hand in his, he looked directly into her eyes. *Do I tell her how I feel?* he thought, but decided against it. "Rodi," he said softly. "We knew this wasn't going to be easy. I spun Roussos a yarn about my own mum so if you go now and tell him something different, he will smell a rat that isn't there. You didn't want the hotel staff to know what you were doing and I honoured that. It was Roussos who heard you talking to the Bressons, otherwise your name would never have been mentioned—well, not by me at that stage."

"I know and I'm sorry," she told him. "I feel so frustrated at the moment. My head tells me to carry on doing what we are doing, you know, the step by step sensible approach, but my heart wants it all to be done yesterday. I just need some tangible evidence of where to go next. There must be somebody who knows where they are."

"And we'll find them; we will," Jake said to reassure her, but his mind was elsewhere and not a million miles away from where he was sitting so close to the girl with whom he was falling so desperately in love. *I love you, Rodi Bartlett,* he said silently. *I want to tell you, but I'm afraid you will think it will interfere with our mission. Maybe when the time is right, I'll let you know. I think you like me...oh God give me the courage and the wisdom to do what is right.*

He was brought out of his reverie by Rodi's cry. Tears ran down her cheeks and she sobbed openly.

"What is it, babe?" Jake asked as he cupped her face in his hands.

"Petros Demetriou," she cried. "He met with such a tragic death when he was distraught and looking for his wife..."

Jake took her in his arms and whispered as she clung to him like a frightened child. "But that was so long ago, sweetheart. How do we know what was going on inside his head, or what had been going on in his marriage?"

Rodi continued to weep. "I know all that, but he was..." She paused poignantly. "...he was my grandfather."

Jake didn't have anything to say that would console Rodi. He just held her close until the tears subsided.

The entry in her journal that night was full of conflicting emotions—elation and bitter disappointment, happiness and sadness and ending with the question, *am I ever going to find my father?*

~ * ~

Jake slept on the sofa that night so Rodi wouldn't feel alone. His determination not to ruin the close friendship they had formed made him keep his true feelings to himself. When she appeared in her pyjamas the following morning, bleary eyed and with tousled hair, he wanted desperately to hold her, caress her, tell her he loved her. "Good morning," he said with a smile. "Did you sleep well?"

"I did," she replied. "I must have been exhausted."

"You were and I think you were emotionally drained yesterday," he answered.

"How about you? Did you sleep well? I know what you said about sofas," she said with a grin as she went to the pantry to find what they might have for breakfast.

"I didn't sleep well," he said, "but I decided we should both go and confront Roussos together. Stick to my story and then he won't be suspicious."

"What shall we say about my involvement?" Rodi asked. "Orange juice, eggs and toast?"

"Oh yes, we'll tell Roussos he can have orange juice, eggs and toast and I think he'll certainly be delighted!" Jake quipped.

Rodi laughed. "Sorry. Confusion of thoughts. Breakfast got a bit mixed up with Roussos...perish the thought," she said light-heartedly. "Well?"

"Well what?" Jake asked, confused himself now.

"Breakfast."

"Orange juice, eggs and toast sounds delicious so long as I have coffee first," he said. "I'll make the coffee and toast."

"Boiled, scrambled, or fried?" she continued.

"Poached," he said with a wink. "I'm only joking. Whatever you prefer, babe. I like eggs any way."

"Back to Roussos, though. What do we say is my part in all this?" she asked seriously. "After all, he heard me asking about Cory Demetriou first."

"Just let me do the talking," Jake instructed. "I'll tell him you were acting on my behalf, because we are..."

"What?" she asked, her eyes wide with curiosity.

"Because we are friends," he said quickly. "You don't mind that, do you?"

"Of course I don't mind," she assured him. "You are the best friend I have. I can't imagine any of my friends back home giving up their break to go tramping around Greece to find somebody they have never met, with somebody they have only known for a few months." She stopped abruptly as the realisation hit her and she asked herself, *Am I being naïve here?* Suddenly she felt her cheeks burning and she fumbled with the plates to hide her embarrassment.

"What's wrong, Rodi?" Jake asked as he realised she was suddenly appearing to be nervous, completely out of character for the confident, self-composed young woman he had first met.

Rodi coughed self-consciously as she placed the plates on the table. "Nothing wrong... I hope," she said quietly, "but it depends what you consider wrong."

"Now you have me nervous," Jake told her. "You're not having second thoughts about it, are you?"

"No, I'm not, but..." Rodi found herself at a loss for words. *How stupid can I be? He's been nothing but the perfect gentleman, so am I misinterpreting his actions? What do I say?* "Can I be totally honest with you, Jake?"

Jake was taken aback. "Of course, you can. What would be the point of not telling the truth?"

"Do you like me?"

Jake felt his face redden and he looked at the floor while he composed himself. "Of course I like you. We're best mates, aren't we?"

Rodi struggled to find the words. "Yes we are, but we are behaving like love-struck teenagers, afraid that if one of us discloses our feelings, the other will run a mile."

Feeling he had been given the green light, Jake gained in confidence. He stood up, took a deep breath and began. "Rodi Bartlett," he said as though he were about to deliver an oratory. "I am madly in love with you, but I am aware that you have a boyfriend back home and I will not come between you and him. It will be difficult for me just to be your friend, but I'll do it, because...I love you." He was pacing the floor, but he turned to face her and looked her directly in the eyes to gauge her reaction. "Will you still allow me to be your friend knowing that?"

Rodi laughed.

"Please don't laugh at me," Jake said. "I'm baring my soul here."

"I'm not laughing at you," she told him. "I'm laughing with relief that you still want to be my friend and there's something I haven't told you. Matthew and I parted company a couple of weeks ago. I couldn't see the point of trying to hold down a long distance relationship with everything that was going on. Funny thing was, when I told him, I was relieved. He'd been cheating on me anyway, and I didn't care. I think that was because I am here..." She paused and looked at him endearingly. "...with you."

Jake sighed with relief. "Does it bother you that I'm in love with you?" he asked bluntly. "I won't expect anything, I promise. Please don't send me away."

Rodi walked around the table until she was in front of him. She cupped his face in her hands and looked into his eyes. "You have done this several times to me in my hour of need to reassure me you were with me all the way. Now I can return the compliment and admit to myself what I have been too blind to see until now." She kissed him tenderly; a long, loving, sensuous kiss and he responded in kind.

"Does this mean we are an item?" Jake asked longingly. "I truly didn't expect that."

Rodi nodded and smiled. "We still have a mountain to climb though, but it will be easy to cope now we have sorted out how we feel about each other."

"I love you, Rodi Bartlett."

"I love you too, Jake Saunders."

~ * ~

They went to meet Stavros Roussos after breakfast. He was in the cellar stocktaking when they arrived. Gaining permission from the bar manager, they descended the stairs into the cellar and found the man sitting on a crate about to light a cigarette.

"If I fully understand the rules of hotel management correctly, I would say that smoking isn't allowed down here," Jake said as they approached him.

Quickly pushing the pack of cigarettes into his pocket, Roussos glared and said brusquely, "What you know?" in his broken English. "What you want?"

Rodi nudged Jake to remind him to keep his cool. "Do you remember I asked you about Cory Demetriou last week?" Jake asked as light-heartedly as he could muster.

Roussos grimaced. "Yes, but you say you not want I know. And why she here?" he asked gesturing towards Rodi.

"Rodi's here because she's with me. Do you have a problem with that?" Jake said pointedly. "Do you really know where Cory Demetriou is? It would make my job so much easier if you did."

Roussos shrugged. "I might," he said, "but like I said..."

"I'm not giving you money, Roussos. Why do you have to ask for money?" Jake asked.

"It important for you, so I have—how you say—valuable information. How valuable for you?" Roussos continued.

"Not so valuable that I'd pay for it," Jake told him and Rodi grabbed hold of his arm to signal that she'd pay if she had to. "Please wait a minute, babe." He took Rodi's hand and made for the door.

"Offer him something," Rodi whispered urgently.

"No," Jake whispered back. "I'm calling his bluff."

Roussos stood up from the crate on which he was perched and began to remove the packet of cigarettes from his pocket. Tapping a cigarette out into his hand, he placed it in his mouth and lit up. Blowing the smoke out around his head, he glanced towards the door. "Go to Halkidiki," he called under his breath, "Then go to hell; I not care."

Seven

They planned to head for northern Greece. "I can't believe we are actually following a lead we don't know is true, or not," Rodi stated. "Are you sure he's not sending us on a wild goose chase?"

Jake was matter-of-fact. "When I went back to ask where we should go in Halkidiki, he seemed quite repentant. He said he was sorry for being..." He paused while he mimicked Roussos. "*How you say—not nice.* I got the sense he didn't want you to dislike him, but that could just be my interpretation of his change of mind. He then told me to go to Mount Athos, because he'd heard a rumour from his uncle that after the terrible accident, the boy, Cory, had gone there. I don't know what's there, except a monastery; well, several monasteries actually."

"A monastery? Why would we go to a monastery, Jake? It's madness."

Jake was thoughtful. "Think about it, Rodi. When Cory Demetriou lost his father, and his mother and sister had disappeared without a trace, he might have found it necessary to withdraw from the world. It would be a lot for a young man to take," he explained. "I do know that many Greek people go on pilgrimages to Mount Athos, but no females are allowed to go in the monasteries."

"So why are we going?" Rodi asked, totally confused by the way things were turning out. "The whole thing makes me feel uncomfortable with the thought that my father might have become a monk. How would I deal with that, Jake? How would *he* deal with the fact that he has a daughter? I almost feel like giving up."

"You can't give up," Jake interrupted. "If Roussos is telling the truth and we find him at Mount Athos, we'll decide then what to say and do. At least you will meet him and fulfil your mum's request."

"How can I meet him if no women are allowed there?" Rodi cried in desperation.

"I'll go and make enquiries first," Jake suggested, "and then if he's there, I'll request that he obtain a pass to come and meet you. They must have something in place for such eventualities."

"That's if he wants to," Rodi said. "Oh Jake, I feel so helpless." Tears began to flow again and Jake held her close to show his total support, his affection and his unwavering love.

~ * ~

As they sat in the plane heading for Thessaloniki, Rodi began to relax. "Maybe we can have a little holiday in Halkidiki," she suggested. She flicked through the pages of the in-flight magazine and showed Jake the pictures of the beaches on the peninsula.

"It's November, babe. We'll freeze on the beach," he said laughing. "We could always snuggle up in bed to keep warm though," he added with a twinkle in his eye.

Rodi nudged his arm in mock disapproval and grinned. "We could, but we promised ourselves lots of exploring and sight-seeing on our travels when we aren't playing detectives."

"Don't be flippant, Rodi," Jake admonished. "This isn't a game and well you know it."

Rodi was suitably chastened. "I know," she said, "but you make me feel happy and relaxed and we need to spend some down time together to get to know each other properly."

"I'm all for that," Jake agreed. "Let's go to Mount Athos first and then we'll take a few days' break either to celebrate, or commiserate."

"That's a hard one," Rodi told him. "If my father is a monk, do I celebrate or commiserate, or both?"

"We celebrate finding him and commiserate if needs be that he won't be able to actively be your dad," Jake said cautiously. "Let's not plan that far ahead just yet."

~ * ~

They landed in Thessaloniki early evening and having collected their luggage, took a taxi to a local hotel where they might stay for one night before embarking on their trip to Ouranoupoli. From there they would be able to take a ferry to Mount Athos, but they preferred to do the two hour drive from Thessaloniki to Ouranoupoli in daylight. There was no rush and, after a hectic season working in Corfu, both Rodi and Jake were happy to chill out for a while.

"Do you realise what we are doing?" Jake asked Rodi as they checked in.

"We're checking in the hotel for a night," she replied with more nonchalance than Jake had expected.

He looked directly at her. "Together."

"Y-e-s, together." Rodi looked puzzled. "We are a couple now, aren't we?"

Jake signed for the key and before they took the lift to their room, he led Rodi to the sofa in the reception area. They sat facing each other and he said, "I don't want to overstep the rules of propriety, Rodi. The very reason we are here is because…" He stopped while he silently considered how honest he might be.

Rodi finished the sentence for him. "…because my mother dared to sleep with her holiday lover and became pregnant."

Jake looked affectionately at the girl he loved. He smiled, albeit a half smile. "I didn't want to say it so bluntly."

Rodi squeezed his hand. "Plain fact, darling; the truth, the whole truth and nothing but the truth. I know what you are saying, and I have always loved my mother dearly, but in nineteen fifty-nine, it was very daring, if not immoral, for young girls to sleep with a guy if they weren't engaged at least. I'm of a different era, a different generation and, though I would hate to be considered a loose woman…" She laughed at what she was saying. "…the only way I can show you that I truly love you is to make love with you. I don't think it's wrong and although I can only guess, my mum didn't think it wrong when she made love with Cory Demetriou. She told me he was the only man she had ever loved and I have to believe that."

"But…"

"No buts, Jake. If we are in this for the long haul, I see no reason why we shouldn't be together. There are means to prevent pregnancy these days so you have no need to worry on that score," she told him. "Now, do you still love me after that little sermon?"

"Yes, of course I do," he replied as they grabbed their suitcases and headed for the elevator. "You know," he said as they sped upwards to the fifth floor, "if you wanted to wait until we have been together longer, I won't mind."

Her answer was to kiss him passionately and urgently. When the doors of the elevator slid open on the fifth floor, they broke apart to the applause of the guests waiting to go down to reception. Grinning sheepishly, they took their suitcases and found room five-one-two where they would spend the night together for the first time. However, their carnal instincts took over once they were inside the room, and afterwards, they decided to wander into the city to find a place to eat and have a glass of wine before making sure they had an early night. "We must make an early start in the morning," Jake said. "We'll hire a car for a few days then at least we're not relying on expensive taxi fares."

"Sounds good to me," Rodi agreed.

~ * ~

"I'm Kostas," the assistant in the car rental office introduced himself courteously. "Where do you intend to drive?"

"Just to Ouranoupoli and surrounding area," Jake told him. "And we are going to visit Mount Athos."

"Are you aware that you need special permission to visit the monasteries and you would need to apply for a visa before you can go there?" Kostas informed them. "And ladies are not permitted at all."

Jake assured the gentleman that he knew the rules. "I am trying to locate an old friend whom we think might be in one of the monasteries. The reason is personal and very important. If we are able to find out whether or not he is there, we would be most grateful. Have you any suggestions?"

Kostas sighed. "Not really, as the monks don't often communicate with visitors apart from those who are going on retreat or pilgrimage, or applying to become part of their exclusive community. If you really want to go there, you will have to take the ferry from Ouranoupoli."

"Thanks. That's a start anyway. We have to make some effort to find our man," Jake told him.

The kindly guy smiled. "You realise that the lady will have to wait on the boat while you make your enquiries." He paused as he considered what they might do. "I suggest that when you arrive, you seek out a taxi driver. The monks run a taxi service, a very expensive taxi service, but for a small donation to the monastery, you might be able to ask questions. It might be best for me to organise your visa, but remember, the young lady must stay on the boat so that she will not attempt to communicate with any of the monastic brethren."

"I understand," Rodi assured him, "but will the ferry crew allow that?"

Kostas nodded. "I'm sure you will have no problem," he said with a smile, "and they might even give you refreshments while you wait."

All paperwork completed, they set off to Ouranoupoli. The two hour drive was uneventful and although they were able to stop and admire the views, they were intent upon arriving at their destination so that they might wait for Jake's visa to be delivered.

"I'm so pleased we booked the hotel before we came," Rodi said as they settled in their room. "I just hope the Greek postal system isn't as bad as it is for sending postcards home. My girlfriend, Lisa said my letter to her took three weeks to arrive from Corfu to Worthing."

Jake laughed. "I know. It's always like that. I'll never understand how numerous flights a day arrive in Corfu from all over Europe and yet the mail takes so long to arrive at its destination. It's only a three and a half hour flight to the UK, for goodness sake!"

The next few days were both relaxing and frustrating. They were able to sample the local restaurants and *tavernas*, but the seasonal rain prevented them from exploring the area as much as they would have liked. After three days, they contacted the Hertz office in Thessaloniki to speak to Kostas and find out how much longer it might take to receive the visa.

"I have your visa here," Kostas announced. "It arrived this morning. It would perhaps have been easier for them to send it direct to your hotel, but never mind. I'll bring it myself tonight."

"You don't have to do that," Jake told him. "I'll come and pick it up tomorrow."

"No problem for me," Kostas said. "I'll enjoy the drive out and I'll bring my wife. We might even stay over seeing it's our wedding anniversary."

"Congratulations," Jake said cheerily. "I hope you will at least allow us to buy you dinner. Our thank you for being so kind and helpful."

"That's very kind of you," Kostas replied.

"Our pleasure. See you around eight o'clock."

Dinner with Kostas and Anna was a pleasant affair and when they bade their goodnights, Rodi and Jake were feeling very relaxed, helped by the several glasses of wine they had consumed with their meal.

"I hope you find who you are looking for," Kostas said as they left. "I wish you luck."

"Thank you, Kostas, and nice to meet you, Anna," Rodi said.

Anna smiled graciously and nodded. Her English was limited, but she managed, "Good luck," as they drove off.

The following morning, Rodi and Jake were up early to face whatever Fate held in store. "I'm so nervous," Rodi admitted as they had breakfast. "I'm nervous and excited both at the same time."

"Try to relax, babe," Jake advised. "I know it's a tall order, but we really have to keep an open mind. Let's face it... I might not even get any answers today."

"Or ever," Rodi conceded. "What if the monks aren't allowed to divulge information about members of their community?"

"And there are so many monasteries," Jake added. "How do we know where Cory Demetriou might be?"

Rodi shivered involuntarily. "Don't, Jake. Let's just go. The sooner we know the better. I'll just get my book. I'll have to try to keep occupied while you are away from the boat."

They arrived at the port before nine o'clock. They knew the first ferry left at ten, but the booking office was not open and there was a notice on the door fortunately in both Greek and English. *Ferries to Mount Athos have been suspended from 10 November 1982 until 7 March 1983. Services will resume in spring. In the case of an emergency, please contact Nico Panu at the port office.*

"Oh no!" Rodi cried. "What do we do now? We came all this way for nothing. Surely Kostas could have warned us that the ferries stopped for the winter months."

"What's today?" Jake asked as he looked at the date on his watch. "November 11. What a nuisance! Let's go to the port office and talk to this Nico chap. He might have a solution for us."

"...so is there any way we might go to Mount Athos today?" Jake pleaded.

Nico Panu picked up the phone and dialled. "Demis," he said and the rest of the conversation was in Greek, so apart from the odd word that Jake picked up, they had no idea what was happening. *"Efharistó. Sas doúme se déka leptá." See you in ten minutes.* He replaced the receiver and looked into the desperate eyes of the young couple before him. "You are lucky," he told them with a smile. "My friend Demis has his own boat and will take you to Mount Athos, but it will cost five thousand drachmas."

Rodi looked at Jake, who came in quickly with a currency conversion. "That's about fifty pounds." And then to Nico, "That's return, for both of us?"

Nico nodded amiably. "Do you have your visa?"

"I do and we know that Rodi will have to stay on the boat while I go to see what I can find out," Jake said, unable to keep the excitement out of his tone.

Demis arrived then. Rodi noted that he was a man of about thirty-five, very athletic looking and with an extremely friendly manner. "*Geia*," he greeted them collectively. "*Ti kánete?*" *How are you?*

"Do you speak English?" Rodi asked.

"A little," he replied. "I think you want to go to Mount Athos, yes?"

Rodi was heartened by his reply. "Will it be all right if I stay on the boat while Jake goes ashore? I won't be any trouble."

"Of course," Demis reassured her. "Shall we go? To get there early is best. We'll pay later, yes?"

They went to the jetty and discovered that Demis's boat was indeed a beautiful fifty-eight foot powerboat, the very essence of luxury in Jake's eyes.

"This is fantastic," he said as they jumped aboard.

"You like?" Demis asked.

"I like," Jake reiterated. "Thank you so much for helping us."

"No problem," Demis replied amicably.

Rodi was similarly impressed, but she sat astern while the two guys, the teacher and the pupil, enthused about all things ocean-going.

"Why so important you go to Mount Athos today?" Demis asked.

Jake glanced at Rodi, who nodded her approval to explain briefly why they needed to find Cory Demetriou.

"I'll help." Demis said. "I'll come ashore with you and be—how you say—Greek speaker."

"Interpreter," Jake corrected.

"Ah yes, interpreter. You would like?"

"That would be great," Jake said. "Do you have a visa?"

"This is usually a charter boat so we have visa all the time. Some monks know me, especially ones who drive taxis. We go to Konstamonitou first. That's the nearest monastery to Ouranoupoli. We talk to first monk we see. If not good, we go to Dochiariou. That's the most big church on Mount Athos."

At Konstamonitou, they sailed as near to the jetty as was possible and having made the boat secure, Demis and Jake jumped onto dry land, leaving Rodi to make herself comfortable while they were away.

"Good luck," she called.

"Fingers crossed," Jake called as he waved his temporary goodbye.

Rodi watched as the two men disappeared up the ramp and round the corner out of sight. She wandered aimlessly round the yacht, unable to settle. Her head was full of wild thoughts. *What shall I say when I meet him? How will he react when he sees me? Will he even remember my mum? Will he deny ever having known her? How could I prove he is my father? Aren't monks supposed to be celibate?* Try as she might, she could find no answers. She decided to make a cup of coffee and endeavour to read her book to distract her mind from unanswerable questions. She looked at her watch. They'd been gone an hour already.

~ * ~

Jake could see nobody as they ambled their way to the end of the rough path. Demis told him not to be impatient. "Monks never rush. It is a sign of urgency and stress and monks not like. It not part of their life. We will sit on tree and wait."

They went to the fallen tree and used it as a bench. Jake picked up a few pebbles and aimed at a big rock about ten metres away. Demis did the same.

"I beat you," he said to Jake, who eagerly took on the challenge.

"In your dreams, my friend," he quipped. "You go first. That's how very confident I am." They laughed almost boyishly at their own actions.

When Demis was ahead five hits to four, they heard the sound of a car approaching. "This will be a monk," Demis said. "They see us waiting."

"How can they see us?" Jake asked.

"I not know, but it happen always. Somebody here, monk comes," Demis told him.

The old jalopy pulled up and an old monk got out and approached them. He nodded in greeting, but said nothing.

Demis moved forward. Their conversation was in Greek, but when Jake heard the name Cory Demetriou, he grew excited only to have his hopes dashed when the monk shook his head. He got back in the car and drove off.

"Come," Demis instructed. "To boat."

"What happened? Tell me. What did he say?" Jake asked urgently trying to hide his disappointment.

"He say he not know. We must go to Dochiariou. More monks; more—how you say—papers."

"Records?" Jake enquired.

"Yes, records. We be there in short time. My boat go fast."

Eight

Rodi jumped out of her reverie as she heard the men running back to the boat. She could see Jake waving enthusiastically and she called out excitedly, "Did you find him?"

Disappointment overwhelmed her when she heard that there was nothing gained by stopping at Konstamonitou. "Oh dear," she wailed. "Is it worth going on? It will probably be the same at the next one too."

"Rodi," Jake chastised. "Have faith. The old monk told us to go to Dochiariou as there are more records there. We have to try."

Rodi sighed deeply. "All right, if you say so, but I can't help feeling that Roussos knew exactly what he was doing when he sent us up here. What fools we were to take his word." Her voice was low, her tone completely despondent.

"We mustn't get our hopes up. If we do, we only set ourselves up for disappointment again, Rodi," Jake said as he worked out his strategy for when they arrived at their next destination.

"Rodi?" Demis interrupted curiously. "Is that your real name? I never heard before."

Rodi smiled. "Aphrodite," she said. "It is short for Aphrodite."

Demis smiled broadly. "Ah," he said, "Aphrodite; beautiful Aphrodite, goddess of love and beauty. It suits you and so very Greek."

"Thank you," Rodi replied. "Thank you very much." She squeezed Jake's hand and snuggled in close to him.

"You are my goddess of love and beauty, darling. Always and all ways," he told her and then he sounded more businesslike. "But back to what I must do when we arrive at Dochiariou. When do we think Cory might have arrived at Mount Athos?"

"It must have been after nineteen-fifty-nine/sixty," Rodi worked out. "I was born in nineteen-sixty and Mum was in Corfu the year before. It's a bit vague, but there was no contact at all after that holiday."

"Let's hope the monks kept good records. At least we have a starting point. I wonder if they also keep records of those who go on retreat," Jake wondered out loud. "After all, it's a possibility that your dad just needed to escape for a while."

Rodi smiled. "For me, that would be the preferable scenario. The thought of my father being a religious zealot fills me with dread. How could I ever live up to standards like that?"

Jake gave her a hug. "I know what you mean, babe, but let's not worry about something we don't know and can do nothing about."

~ * ~

Jake and Demis approached the main entrance of the monastery. The path from the jetty this time was more accessible and as they arrived at the main gate, they were asked to show their visas to a young novice monk who stood like a sentry on guard at a royal palace. Demis asked to be directed to the library since it was reputed to have three hundred and ninety-five catalogued manuscripts, as well as forty-six that have not been classified, and one thousand-five hundred printed books. Hopefully, the records would be housed here also.

There was a mystical silence about the place that openly conveyed a very spiritual atmosphere and Jake was overwhelmed with a feeling of awe. "I think I understand why people come here for spiritual sustenance," he whispered to Demis.

Demis shrugged, not because he disagreed, but because he didn't understand what Jake was saying. "Big English words," he whispered in reply and smiled resignedly at his new friend.

The librarian monk was a very serious looking man, but not unapproachable. Jake was about to ask him if he spoke English, when the monk placed his finger to his lips and silently directed them out of the main hall of the library into an ante-room where they might speak freely. Once there, Jake asked again. "Do you speak English?"

"I do," the librarian replied. "How might I be of assistance?"

Jake explained their plight as briefly as possible, finishing with, "It was suggested to Miss Bartlett and me that Cory Demetriou might have come to Mount Athos after the death of his father and the disappearance of his mother and sister."

"One moment," the monk said and he disappeared. Within minutes, he re-appeared with an enormous tome which he placed on the table before them. "What year would that be?" he asked.

"We don't know for sure, but we think it must have been around nineteen fifty-nine or sixty. It might even have been later, but certainly not after nineteen seventy-four. We know his father, Petros Demetriou was killed in an accident and there was no police record of that in Paleocastritsa. The police office there only opened in nineteen seventy-four." Jake was thinking out loud and trying to fit the pieces of the jigsaw together in his head.

The librarian scanned the list of novices entering the monasteries from nineteen fifty onwards. "We have comparatively few novices each year, so the search ought not to be difficult." He traced the list with his finger and came across a novice from Lakones, Corfu who had entered Dionysiou monastery in nineteen fifty-four. "Brother Antonis. I am able to contact him to see if he knows anything of Cory Demetriou, but it will take a few days. I am sure he will know if the man you need ever came here. We try to place pilgrims with monks from the same area, but it is such a long time ago."

Jake felt his heart beating wildly in his chest. Rodi would be ecstatic. "How soon would you know?" he asked.

"A few days," the kindly monk repeated. "Leave me your name and address. I'll have a messenger sent out to Dionysiou and in the meantime, I'll get an eager novice to trawl through the pilgrim visitors' books. That will take a while, but I'm sure it's not beyond the realms of possibility."

"Your English is so good," Jake told him. "Very impressive."

"Today is your lucky day," the librarian said, smiling. "You met the only Anglo-Greek monk on Mount Athos. English mother, Greek father. I was born in Athens, but went to school in England when my father was posted to London. When my mother died, I was just seventeen years old. Father and I returned to Greece. I came on retreat to Mount Athos and never went back to Athens. I found my calling."

"What a beautiful story," Jake said as he wrote his name and the address of the hotel in Ouranoupoli.

"I'm Brother Tymon and good to meet you, Jake. I'll do as much as I can to help your friend find her father. In an odd sort of way, I am pleased he is not here. It would have caused untold problems for him and for her. How long will you be in Ouranoupoli?"

"As long as it takes," Jake assured him. "I promised Rodi we'd spend the rest of our lives searching if we had to."

"Rodi?" Brother Tymon asked.

Jake smiled. "Aphrodite."

"Ah." The monk nodded knowingly.

"Jake!" Demis called from a discreet distance across the room. "We need to leave if we are to get back to Ouranoupoli before dark. I think Rodi worry on the boat alone."

"Ah, she is with you," Brother Tymon said. "You need to go and tell her we will help. Hopefully, she will see the difficulties involved, but we'll try."

Jake shook the monk's hand. "She understands only too well," he said, "but she will be grateful if we make some progress, however small. Thank you so much for your help."

"My pleasure, Jake," Brother Tymon said. "Have a safe trip back to Ouranoupoli and I shall send the message to Dionysiou as soon as you leave."

Jake couldn't hide his smile from ear to ear. "At last something to look forward to," he said to Demis as they raced back to the yacht.

"Don't hope for too much," Demis advised.

"I won't, but I'm not sure how I will keep Rodi's excitement in check." As he spoke, he caught sight of her on the deck, waving madly. He waved back and ran as fast as he could to hold her in his arms and tell her his news.

Nine

The weather took a turn for the worse and the rains came with a vengeance. After three days of sitting around in the hotel and trying to understand Greek television, both Rodi and Jake were becoming frustrated with waiting for news.

"Are you sure he will do as he promised?" Rodi asked.

"I'm as sure as I can be, darling. Brother Tymon is a monk, a man of God, a good man and half-English to boot!" Jake grinned. "How lucky was that? It has to be a good omen."

"I hate this waiting," she wailed. "It's worse than waiting for exam results. I feel so helpless."

Jake understood exactly how she was feeling. "I know, babe. Whatever you feel, I feel. We are in this together, so you must never allow yourself to feel alone. I promised I would search with you if it took the rest of our lives and I meant it."

Rodi smiled at the man with whom she had fallen hopelessly, madly and totally in love. "I love you," she whispered. "Thank you." They held each other close until suddenly there was a loud knocking on the door.

"Letter for Mr Saunders."

Jake jumped up from the sofa and opened the door with a flourish. "Thank you," he said as he took the letter from the porter. He dug deep in his pocket and found a hundred drachma bill which he handed to the deliverer of the letter.

"Thank you, sir," was the happy response.

Rodi was excited. "What did you give him?" she asked.

"A hundred drachmas," Jake said.

"No wonder he was smiling," she told him. "That's a big tip for delivering a letter."

"Worth every *obol*!" he quipped.

"*Obol*?" Rodi questioned.

'It's a sixth of a drachma," he explained. "I once looked up what drachmas were made up of, you know, like pence in a pound, or cents in a dollar, and *obol* was the only thing I could find. That's one little bit of useless information I shall never again find use for, but there you have it. Put it in your memory bank!"

Rodi laughed and Jake handed her the letter. She held it to her heart and shuddered involuntarily. "Me?" she asked him nervously.

"This is all for you, sweetheart," he assured her. "Open it, or we'll never know one way or the other."

With shaking hands, she tore open the envelope and read out loud: "*Dear Rodi and Jake...*You told him my name! Thank you. *I have news for you that may help a little in your search for Cory Demetriou, although you will see when you read what we found out, there will still be hurdles to clear and mountains to climb if you are destined to find him.*

Brother Antonis from Lakones joined the monastery in nineteen fifty-four as we discovered from our records. He tells me he was the schoolboy friend of Cory Demetriou and he actually asked Cory to join him in Dionysiou when he left Lakones at the age of sixteen. Demetriou refused, saying that the monastic life was not for him, although Brother Antonis describes him as a good man. Rodi's eyes filled with tears. "He had to be a good man," she said. "My mum fell in love with him and…well, he had to be good."

She sniffed, but continued. "*Brother Antonis did not hear from him at all for a few years. After all, a novice has to devote all his time to God and to study until the time of his ordination. However, in late nineteen fifty-nine, Demetriou arrived at Dionysiou on retreat and sought out Brother Antonis. He was apparently distraught about the death of his father and the disappearance of his mother and sister. He needed his friend and some spiritual guidance to sustain him in his grief.*

Rodi paused again. "The date is right," she said. "It confirms what was going on when Mum was expecting me. If Mum had written to him at that time, he might never have received the letter, but how can I be sure she did write to him? She was always so adamant that she didn't know where he was."

She continued reading the letter to Jake. "*Demetriou stayed with Brother Antonis for one week. In spite of his personal fulfilment during that time, he still had no desire to take up the life of a monk. Brother Antonis said when his friend left, he was refreshed and eager to begin a new life. Demetriou informed Brother Antonis he would go to Athens and learn how to become a chef like his father had been, but there was something about Demetriou that Brother Antonis could not fathom, something that went beyond his grief, something that had broken his spirit, broken his heart.*

That's as far as we know. Brother Antonis did not hear from Demetriou again, but I think there might be something for you to follow up in Athens.
Good luck.
With kindest wishes,
Tymon"

She sighed deeply and smiled. "Wow," she said. "At last something positive, even though we'll have to go to Athens from here."

Jake gave her a hug. "I almost want to like Roussos now," he said ironically. "He really must have heard something about Cory going to Mount Athos."

"Maybe he thought he'd become a monk," Rodi suggested. "It did seem that Roussos wanted to lead us on what might have been a wasted journey. When monks join an order, I would think they leave all trappings of their former life behind. It's just a thought on my part, but I'm certain Roussos would know that for sure."

"And that thought is irrelevant now," Jake told her. "Let's go out for dinner and plan our next move." He paused deliberately. "And I think a bottle of wine is in order."

~ * ~

They left Halkidiki a couple of days later and flew directly to Athens. They had no idea where to start looking.

"Perhaps there is a Greek equivalent of a Citizens' Advice Bureau," Rodi wondered.

"I have no idea," Jake replied, "but there will be a library and libraries contain all sorts of directories and local information."

Rodi laughed. "Look what happened with the census in Corfu," she stated pointedly. "The Greek language will certainly beat us every time."

"I know, but there'll be somebody there who speaks English," Jake reminded her. "When it comes to speaking foreign languages, we English are very incompetent. Most other Europeans speak English well. I often feel ashamed that I didn't follow up my basic French and Spanish after I left school."

"I studied French and German to advanced level so I'm fairly competent in making myself understood in France and Germany," Rodi told him.

"Well, well, well," he said. "I learn something new about you every day."

"Keeps you interested," she joked. "However, I don't think anybody learns Greek in British schools. We'll have to teach ourselves."

"We?" Jake interrupted. "I don't think I'm capable of learning a new language at my age!"

"Of course you are," Rodi told him. "You're only twenty-seven. That's still young! And anyway, you've picked up the odd word already because you've worked in Corfu for the past five years."

"Point taken, Rodi. We'll try to learn it together when we go back to Paleocastritsa."

Rodi stared at him in horror. "We can't go back yet," she cried. "We need to keep looking for my dad."

Jake took her hand. "Baby," he said gently. "I mean next summer. Our jobs are secure and we'll have to top up the coffers to finance our search. We can't give up work much as we want to devote our time to this search."

Rodi nodded slowly. "I know that, but I've been thinking I'll have to go back to Worthing too sometime. Maybe we can both go home for Christmas."

"Sounds good to me," Jake agreed. "First of all, though, let's find the public library here and see what information it holds. With Christmas only four weeks away, we have a lot to do before then."

They were once again confronted with documents they could not read. With the assistance of yet another librarian, they learned that the only food technology college in Athens at that time was attached to the School of Arts.

"In the nineteen sixties, it was at a time when vocational studies were developing in Greece and a good time to take advantage of the training on offer for lots of trades," the librarian told them. "If you go to the School of Arts, they should have all records of students from when the college opened." She gave them the address and directed them to take a taxi as being the easiest and quickest way to get there.

~ * ~

"Cory Demetriou," the bursar read from the college records. "Enrolled in January nineteen sixty to study hotel management. Qualified with honours in June nineteen sixty-four." He paused as he continued to search the pages of yet another book of recorded information. "Gained a position in the Electra Hotel as under-manager. In those days, a very good job."

"Is the hotel still there?" Rodi asked.

"It is, but now called Hotel Acropolista. Not far from here. Turn left out of here and walk for two blocks. The hotel is across the junction on the corner of Mikonos Street," the bursar informed them. "I have to say it is very unlikely Cory Demetriou will still work there. It isn't normal for trainees to stay in one hotel, but they may still have staff records from sixteen years ago." He smiled kindly. "Good luck."

"Thank you so much," Rodi and Jake chorused in unison as they left with a definite spring in their step.

The manager of the hotel wasn't available, but his assistant asked if he might help. "Do you want to make a reservation?" he asked as he reached for the ledger.

"No, thank you," Rodi said politely. "My name is Rodi Bartlett and I am trying to trace my father who once worked here."

"Oh I see," the assistant manager said warily and both Rodi and Jake picked up on his uncertainty.

"The bursar at the School of Arts sent us here," Jake explained. "He seemed to think you might still have Rodi's father's name in your staff records and perhaps where he went when he left here."

The gentleman coughed. "This is very unusual," he said, seemingly feeling very uncomfortable. "Do you have proof that you are related to the person you are looking for? It would be very unwise of me to hand out personal information to anybody who asks. I must check with my superior before I start to look at our records."

Rodi's heart was beating wildly in her chest. "I don't have his name on my birth certificate if that's what you want," she said in a panic.

Jake grabbed her arm and signalled to her to slow down. "We can provide some proof if required."

"How?" Rodi snapped.

"We have proof," Jake told the gentleman who wasn't making their task easy. "When will your superior be available? May we make an appointment to speak with him personally? We don't wish to cause any problems for you, or for him. You have our word on that."

Rodi smiled at Jake. *Thank you, darling,* she thought. *What would I do without you? You always have a sensible, calm and reassuring attitude when I lose it.*

The assistant manager smiled. "I do not wish to be difficult either," he said. "I'm Tony Vlakhos and the manager of the hotel is Galen, my brother. He won't be back on duty until tomorrow. Perhaps you might come back at nine o'clock in the morning with your proof of identity and I will make a note in his diary that you wish to meet with him."

"Thank you. That will be great," Jake replied.

"What is the name of the gentleman you wish to contact?" Vlakhos asked.

Rodi looked first at Jake for reassurance and then directly at Vlakhos. "Cory Demetriou," she said confidently. "He is my father."

When they were out of the hotel Rodi turned to Jake. "Proof?" she asked pointedly. "Where on earth am I going to get proof? My father's name is not on my birth certificate."

"But you have your mother's will, don't you?" Jake reminded her. "Last will and testament and all that."

Rodi felt her cheeks burn with embarrassment. She sighed with relief. "God bless you, Jake Saunders," she exclaimed and this time she said out loud, "What would I do without you?"

The rest of the day was spent wandering around Athens taking in the sights and absorbing the atmosphere of the city steeped in ancient history. They climbed the high, rocky outcrop overlooking the city to the Acropolis and marvelled in the glory of the Parthenon, the most well-known of the historical architectural remains atop this ancient hill.

"This is probably the best time of the year to come up here," Jake commented as he took a photograph of Rodi in front of the ancient monument, majestic still in spite of its antiquity. "Imagine having to climb that hill in summer with the sun blazing down on us."

"Mind you," Rodi rejoined, "We would perhaps have a better view of the city in summer without all this low cloud. Still, it's an experience I shall always treasure."

~ * ~

The following morning they were up bright and early, eager to meet Galen Vlakhos and seriously hoping he might have the information that would lead them to Cory Demetriou.

"Good morning," Rodi greeted the gentleman behind the desk. "We are here to see Galen Vlakhos."

"One moment, madam," the receptionist said cordially. "I'll see if he is available." She turned and disappeared into an office alongside the reception desk.

Rodi felt irritated and her thoughts were less then sociable. *He is available. We were given an appointment.* She looked at Jake with nothing less than exasperation in her expression.

The receptionist returned smiling. "Mr Vlakhos will be out in a few minutes. Please take a seat while you wait."

Rodi held on tightly to Jake's hand and stared at the office door from whence the receptionist had come. Without averting her gaze, she whispered, "Why does everything take so long? Can't they see how urgent it is?"

Jake gave her a playful nudge. "Rodi, you were definitely at the back of the queue when they handed out patience. I think they'd run out of supplies when they got to you!" he whispered in her ear. "Mr Vlakhos cannot possibly know how important this is for you. Calm down, baby. He'll be here soon."

When the telephone rang, they were both startled, but watched the receptionist with eager eyes. "Mr Vlakhos will see you now," she called. "Please come this way."

Inside the tiny office, Galen Vlakhos, a man of some maturity, rose to greet them warmly. "How are you?" he asked amicably. "Your names, please?"

"I'm Rodi Bartlett and this is my..." She paused wondering how she should introduce Jake. Throwing caution to the wind, she continued, "...my partner, Jake Saunders."

Jake smiled happily and shook the manager's hand. "Pleased to meet you, sir."

"And how can I help you?" Vlakhos asked.

"I understood that your brother would have explained the situation to you," Rodi said again, trying to hide her irritation.

Vlakhos smiled again. "Yes, he did, but I wish to make sure he had...how you English say...got the right end of the stick. The story is very unusual."

"Start at the beginning, Rodi," Jake urged. "You really have nothing to hide."

Rodi held on to her mother's will as she related as much of the story as she was able, including the recent information from Brother Tymon and the bursar from the School of Arts. "Please understand that all this is new to me too," Rodi admitted shyly as she handed the will across the desk to Galen Vlakhos. "I had no idea who my father was until last year. I really hope you are able to help me find him; at least point me in the right direction."

Vlakhos studied the codicil of the will and then handed it back to Rodi. "I have to say that I feel your mother's sincerity in what she wrote. Let me see what I can do," he said. He handed Rodi a piece of paper and instructed her to read what was on it. "I took the liberty of writing it in English."

Both Rodi and Jake laughed. "Thank you so much," she said light-heartedly. "You are either psychic, or you were a fly on the wall in the Corfu library and here in Athens, seeing us struggling with the Greek alphabet."

Vlakhos laughed with them and signalled to Rodi to read what she had been given.

She read slowly and silently. *Cory Petros Demetriou—Under-manager 1964-1970. Duties included sous chef; kitchen organisation; supplies; general hotel management; reservations and staff rosters. Competent and proficient in all aspects of hospitality.*

Resigned April 1970 after gaining a position as hotel manager in Protaras, Cyprus.

Rodi sighed and looked first at Jake and then Galen Vlakhos. "This is wonderful," she said, "but Cyprus? We can't possibly go there before Christmas and do we know which hotel, Mr Vlakhos?"

Jake leaned over to squeeze her hand for reassurance. "Rodi, it's another step forward. Don't try to run before you can walk. We'll talk about it when we've had time to let all this sink in. It would be senseless to go to Cyprus without first making enquiries."

Vlakhos smiled at them both. "It must be so frustrating for you, but like Mr Saunders says, it is a step in the right direction. I do not have the name of the hotel, but I suggest you contact the immigration department in Nicosia. There will be records there of all immigrants allowed entry into Cyprus in nineteen seventy. I think they might also have information of where those people found work."

"Thank you very much, Mr Vlakhos," Rodi said. "I really appreciate your trouble."

"My pleasure, Rodi," he told her. "And Rodi...?"

"Yes?"

"Lovely unusual name." He smiled again and wished them good luck. "I hope you are able to find your father. Every girl needs her dad."

Ten

The flight from Athens to London Gatwick airport seemed long and tedious. It was a week before Christmas and the biting British winter winds nipped at their faces as soon as they stepped from the aircraft. They took a taxi to Rodi's house in Worthing, having asked her friend, Lisa, to remove the dust sheets and turn on the central heating the day before their arrival.

"I'm so pleased to be home," Rodi said as she removed her coat and threw it over the banister. Almost as soon as it landed, she retrieved it and hung it on a peg in the cloakroom under the stairs. "Mum always told me off for leaving my coat on the banister," she explained. "Conscience kicked in just then."

Jake gave her a hug. "And would she approve of having me to stay?" he asked with a wry smile.

"You know what?" she said wistfully. "I don't really know if she would approve or not, but she believed in love and if she's up there looking down on me, she'll feel the love we share and give her approval whole-heartedly. I truly believe that."

"I love you, Rodi Bartlett," Jake told her longingly. "More than you'll ever know."

"I do know, Jake. Everything we feel for each other is right and that's all we need to consider, isn't it?"

"Not quite all," Jake said pointedly. "My family has no idea I'm back in England. The last time we spoke, I told them I would be away for Christmas."

Automatically, Rodi picked up the phone and heard the dialling tone. Immediately, she gasped. "What the...?"

"What's up," Jake asked.

"I've got a dialling tone. I know I asked to be cut off when I went away," she explained. "I didn't want to pay line rental when I wasn't here to take calls and apart from that, I didn't want the telephone to be ringing out in an empty house. It really worries me that BT didn't cut me off."

Jake picked up a note left by the phone that Rodi had missed. He read out loud. *Welcome home, Rodi and Jake. Took the liberty of calling BT to connect you again. New number - 416944. Thought you'd need the phone. See you soon, I hope. Love, Lisa xx*

"What a friend," Rodi acknowledged. "She thinks of everything. Make your call, sweetheart. I'll put the kettle on and please say we'll go north to visit whenever it's convenient for them. Later I'll phone Eva and Jean-Paul to tell them where we are up to with our search."

Jake held the phone away from his ear as his mother shrieked at the sound of his voice. "Where are you, darling?" she asked.

"I'm in Worthing."

"What on earth are you doing in Worthing? Or perhaps I should ask..." Molly Saunders' voice tailed off before she finished her question.

Jake felt his cheeks burning. "Can I call you back in about an hour?" he asked. "There's something I must do and it's urgent."

"Okay," his mother said, "but I think you are avoiding telling me something, Jake Saunders."

"Later, Mum." He replaced the phone on the cradle and went into the kitchen to join Rodi.

~ * ~

"But why haven't you told them about me?" Rodi asked. "I don't know what to think, Jake. It isn't as though we've run off and got married."

Jake sighed. "And thank goodness for that," he said. "It's because my marriage didn't work out that they've all become extremely protective of me."

Rodi sighed too. "You are twenty-seven years old, Jake. Surely they know you are old enough to make your own choices and make your own mistakes too."

"I'm sorry, babe," he told her with deep emotion in his voice. "I know I should stand up to them more, but I was so devastated when Carla left me for some jerk in her office and my family rallied round to pick up the pieces. They didn't approve when I married her, but went along with it because I thought I was in love.

"Now I'm in love with you…I realise what love is. I was just flattered that Carla, the most attractive girl around, agreed to go out with me. I didn't think I stood a chance with her so I asked her to marry me after only four weeks. She jumped at the chance because she thought my parents were wealthy. She came from the lower end of town and it showed. As far as I was concerned, I just saw the beautiful girl who wanted to sleep with me. I was only eighteen and desperate for sex—rampant teenage hormones." He laughed. "I was ready to elope and told my parents if I couldn't persuade them to go along with my wedding plans, I would do just that. With hindsight, I don't think I would have eloped anyway, but it worked and at the time, I was delighted."

Rodi took his hand. "How naïve of you, Jake," she said tenderly. "Naïve and sneaky, but I can't believe you would be so ruled by what's inside your pants—not you, the person who debated for months whether or not to tell me how you felt."

Jake was embarrassed. "I have to admit I feel like an idiot now," he conceded, "and I also admit that meeting you has given me much more confidence in dealing with what might come when I tell my parents about you. The whole reason for working in Corfu was to maintain my independence. That's why I'm so happy there. I don't have to be smothered by my parents and older brother."

Rodi smiled. "That's what parents do, Jake," she said. "They are only looking after their little boy."

"You're right there, babe," he agreed. "That's exactly how they regard me—their little boy. At home, they were unwittingly shattering my confidence. That's what I've had all my life, because I was an afterthought! My mother was forty-two when she had me, which meant my brother was twenty-one years older than me. It was like having three parents, a pain in the backside at times."

"You'll just have to let them know you're a big boy now."

"I know and I've tried, but they always look so hurt when I stand up to them," Jake explained. "I hate hurting their feelings, but..." He paused significantly. "...when they meet you, they'll be captivated by the wonderful choice I've made this time. I know it."

~ * ~

"That's settled then," Jake told her after he had spoken with his parents. "We go to Rivington the day after Boxing Day."

Rodi gave him a hug. "Are they all right with it?"

"It?"

"Well, with me then," Rodi asked.

"They are fine," he reassured her. "I gave you a wonderful reference and Mum's parting words were, *'if you're as happy as you sound, son, then we're happy too.'* They'll love you, I know."

"Thank you," she said, "but Jake?"

"Yes?"

"You haven't told them about my search, have you?" Rodi asked. "I really would like to keep that just between us at the moment."

"I haven't said anything on that score, babe. Don't worry." Jake paused before he continued. "But what will you say if they ask about your family? It could be an innocent enquiry on their part."

Rodi thought before she spoke. "I'll tell the truth, but maybe watered down a bit. I would never lie, Jake. They might not approve of our running from country to country looking for my missing father."

"I know what you mean, darling," he agreed. "But please don't think I would be ruled by what they might think. I made you a promise and I'll stand by my word."

"Thanks, sweetheart," she said with relief. "But I do want to put the search for Cory Demetriou on the back burner for a while. We need some you-and-me time."

Jake grinned from ear to ear. "I couldn't agree more."

~ * ~

With shopping complete, presents bought and wrapped, Christmas tree dressed and turkey ready to put in the oven before they went to bed on Christmas Eve, Rodi and Jake snuggled on the sofa and watched *The Wizard of Oz* on television. They laughed when they discovered they had both watched the film on Christmas Eve for more years than they could remember.

"Hopefully the BBC or ITV might change their plans and show a different film one year," Rodi said. "If it's not this, it's *The Sound of Music* and I love both films, but I think I could sing every song and speak every part without being prompted I've seen them so many times!"

By eleven o'clock they were both falling asleep on the sofa. "Time for bed," Jake announced. "We have to give Santa time to bring our presents. I'll just put the turkey in the oven. It is going to be so tender and succulent in the morning. Cooking it at a very low temperature always works."

"Since when have you become so domesticated?" Rodi asked.

"Since I asked Mum how to cook a turkey the first Christmas with my ex, because Carla never cooked anything," Jake explained.

"Aw, poor baby," Rodi said sympathetically. "I wish I'd met you before she did."

"But if that were the case, we might not be here now, sweetheart. I always think Fate has a lot to do with how our lives pan out," he said philosophically. "I don't believe our lives are planned. We're all masters of our own destiny. Sometimes we are helped along the way by unsuspecting people who cross our paths, but ultimately we have to be in charge."

Rodi smiled and gave the man in her life a hug. She held him close and whispered in his ear. "I love you. Jake Saunders, and if I regard that fact with your philosophy on life, I have to think if my mum hadn't died, we would never have met."

"Please don't say that, Rodi."

"I'm just being philosophical like you," she said quietly. "On the surface, it looks like Mum died and enabled us to meet. Maybe that's true to a point, but none of us has control over cancer. We can philosophise all we like, but the big C won't listen. In that respect, co-incidence has played a part too."

Jake sighed. "Darling, let's not get too maudlin on Christmas Eve. I want you to be happy."

"I am happy," she reassured him, "and Mum would be happy too, I know."

~ * ~

They welcomed Christmas Day by making passionate love and experiencing unbounded adoration for each other. They wandered downstairs in dressing gowns and slippers, deciding to open their presents after breakfast. Jake seemed on edge and Rodi noticed. "What's wrong, babe?" she asked him. "You look as though you have the worries of the world on your shoulders. I hope you aren't concerned about going to visit your folks the day after tomorrow."

"Of course not," he said, with more confidence. He was thinking of the looming task he had to keep secret until after breakfast.

"Come on then, love," Rodi encouraged. "Smile! It's Christmas!"

They took their coffee into the lounge and Rodi began giving Jake her presents.

"Socks and undies?" he asked cheekily.

"Be careful, Mr Saunders, or I'll take them back and get a refund!" she quipped. "Just open them and then you can play Santa for me."

Jake couldn't stop grinning. "Sun glasses! Just what I need in the snow!" He laughed and Rodi laughed with him.

"I know you need them for next season. Your others are taped up with Sellotape," she reminded him. "I can't have my man looking as though nobody owns him!"

"Thanks, baby," he said as he opened the next one. It was long and triangular and felt very solid. "Now I wonder what this can be."

"Well, if you don't like it, I'll have it, cos it's my favourite," Rodi told him. "And anyway, I only bought it because I knew you would share it with me."

"Just for that, I'll eat it all myself. Toblerone is my favourite too," he said light-heartedly. "That's something else we have in common."

After opening an array of lovely little gifts—socks, aftershave, a book of crosswords, and a 1983 diary, Rodi handed him a gift she wanted to save until last.

"Another one?" he asked, genuinely surprised.

"I saved the best till last," she said. "I hope you like it."

Jake tore open the wrapping, eager to see what Rodi had given him. "A Rolex watch?" he said, dismayed. "Rodi, this is too much."

Rodi went and sat beside him. "Confession time," she announced. "Mum was left that watch by her father, my grandfather whom I never really knew. She told me that when I found the man I truly wanted to spend the rest of my life with, I should give it to him."

Jake gasped. "Oh Rodi…"

Rodi smiled lovingly at him. "Wear it with my love, darling. Merry Christmas."

"I will treasure it always and thank you, baby. I love you with all my heart."

"I love you too."

Jake searched under the tree for his most important gift for Rodi. "I am giving you the best first," he said. "You have given me no alternative." He handed a present about the size of a shoe box to Rodi, who opened it eagerly only to find yet another box inside that one and yet another box inside the next and the next, seemingly *ad infinitum.* "You are teasing me, Jake Saunders," she said, but kept on opening box upon box until she found the smallest one at the end. "And what have we here?" she asked.

Jake took the tiny box from her. "Allow me," he said as he removed the Christmas wrapping and opened it to reveal the most exquisite diamond solitaire ring she had ever seen. He knelt before her. "Will you marry me, Rodi?"

Tears trickled down her cheeks. "Are you serious?" she asked.

"Of course I'm serious. I've never loved anybody like I love you. You are my world, my life. Please say you will do me the honour of becoming my wife."

"Yes, yes, yes," she cried and smothered him with kisses. She paused significantly. "But there is one condition, darling."

"Name it," Jake said. "There is nothing that will interfere with how I feel about you."

Rodi held him tightly and looked directly into his eyes. "I will marry you when my father can walk me down the aisle."

"Done deal, baby."

They spent the rest of Christmas Day nineteen eighty-two revelling in each other's company and basking in each other's love.

Eleven

They drove north the day after Boxing Day as planned. Fortunately, the threatened snow did not fall and the daytime temperatures were unseasonably high—well, if eight degrees Celsius might be considered high. Rodi threw the keys of her VW Golf to Jake saying, "You drive, Jake. You know the way and I think I'm too nervous to drive on the M25 and M6."

"No problem, sweetheart," Jake replied as he caught the keys. "I think I'll enjoy driving on British roads again. At least they have decent surfaces!"

The visit to Jake's parents' house went well, apart from a little awkwardness when Rodi answered the question about her mother. "She was a single mother and she passed away last year."

"What about your father?" Molly Saunders asked. "Do you ever see him?"

Jake was quick to intervene. "What is this, Mum? An interrogation?"

Patrick Saunders joined in. "Slow down, Molly. We don't want to scare her off. She's only been here five minutes, so she has."

"Not at all," his mother replied. "I'm just getting to know Rodi...that's such an unusual name. Where does it come from?"

Explanation over, Rodi tried to ease Mrs Saunders's mind. "I never knew my father, but when Mum died, there was information in her will that told me he is Greek. Eventually, I hope to contact him, but not just yet."

Jake smiled at Rodi's honesty.

Mrs Saunders wiped away a tear that involuntarily trickled down her cheek. "I hope you find him, Rodi," she said kindly, "and I hope my Jake will help you. That's the saddest story I have ever heard. Every girl needs her dad and every dad needs to know his daughter. It will perhaps be a shock to him, but he'll love you when he meets you. I just know he will."

A week later after having celebrated the coming of nineteen eighty-two, they were travelling back to Worthing and Jake commented on his parents' attitude towards Rodi. "I can't believe how laid back they were, babe," he said with a huge smile on his face. "If you'd seen them when I introduced Carla, you would know what a massive transformation has taken place."

Rodi smiled at him. "It's not really the same circumstances, Jake," she said wryly.

"I know, but I'm just so happy for us and for them too," he continued. "Even Jonathan and Trisha fell over themselves to make you feel welcome. The kids too. I'm so happy."

Rodi nudged him playfully. "I think your brother and his wife are simply pleased they don't have to look after you anymore. Gregory and Danielle are just sweet kids. Not all teenagers create such a good first impression. I hope they stay as close as they are now. Twins usually have that special bond."

"I'm sure they will," Jake said, thinking of his nephew and niece with great affection. "Am I allowed to say I told you so?"

"You told me what?" Rodi asked

"That they'd all love you almost as much as I do," he told her.

She smiled at her fiancé and snuggled as close as she might as he drove along the Worthing promenade just minutes away from home.

~ * ~

"How soon do we have to be back in Corfu?" Rodi asked when, at the end of January, they were thinking about writing to the immigration department in Nicosia.

"We need to book our flights before Easter," Jake informed her. "Easter Sunday is April the eleventh this year, quite late, so we can perhaps go early March in order to settle in before we have to start work."

"That's fine by me," she replied. "I put a retainer on the apartment, so we won't have to look for somewhere to live. With both of us paying the rent, it will be much more financially viable for us. But I've been thinking..."

"Just be careful, Rodi!" he quipped. "That could be dangerous!"

Ignoring his blatant disregard for her seriousness, she continued. "Mum left me a substantial amount of money when she died so I have—*we* have no financial worries."

Jake stopped her mid-sentence. "Hold on a minute, Rodi. That's your money not mine and you really don't have to tell me about it just now. I have saved a substantial amount too while I've been working in Corfu. The past five years have treated me kindly, so..."

Rodi took his hand. "I would like to tell you, because it affects our future together."

"But..."

"No buts, Jake. Just listen and then you can tell me what you think." She settled on the settee in front of the fire and pulled Jake down to sit beside her. "I'm going to sell this house..."

"What?" Jake gasped.

"Stop interrupting and just listen," she told him. "I have thought long and hard about this, even before I left for Corfu last spring. It isn't a rash decision, but I didn't mention it previously because I wanted to make sure I was doing the right thing for myself. It had to be my decision, but now I want to share it with you."

Jake sighed and squeezed the hand of this remarkable young woman whom he loved with all his heart.

Rodi continued. "I love Corfu—maybe it's in my blood—and I want to live there."

Jake raised his eyebrows questioningly, but said nothing.

"Keeping this house is an unnecessary expense for me and even though I have no mortgage, I still have to pay my rates and all the other financial demands owning a house involves. I worry in case there is a burst water pipe, or storm damage while I'm in Corfu and there's always the risk of a break-in when the house is left unattended for months on end. I could rent it out, but I would still be responsible for anything that goes wrong. How on earth would I sort out tenants' problems when I am so far away?" She looked at Jake to see if she might gauge his opinion on what she had just disclosed.

"I don't know what to say, Rodi," he said. "Are you absolutely sure this is what you want to do? It's a massive step to take." He paused and shook his head slowly, but the gentle smile on his lips told Rodi he wouldn't condemn her decision. "Now I know why we have to learn to speak Greek!"

"Does that mean you'll live with me in Corfu?" she asked.

He grinned. "I'd live with you in Timbuktu if that's what you wanted, but..."

"Oh, Jake, no buts—please," she pleaded.

"Come on, babe, he said pointedly. "This is an enormous decision. We have to weigh up the pros and cons before we sign on the dotted line. Are you sure it isn't Cory Demetriou who is the driving force in all this?" He said it gently. "I'm not pouring cold water on it and there's nothing I would like more than to live in Corfu with you by my side, but are you thinking about your father, or of us?"

Rodi felt tears trickling down her cheeks. She took a deep breath and spoke softly, but with undisguised confidence. "Both," she said. "You wanted pros and cons, well, I can supply all the pros, but at this moment in time, I can see no cons. The only con I might have had was if you refused point blank to live there permanently. As for pros...number one, the summer weather; two, dream jobs; three, relaxed life-style; four, being able to buy land easily to build our family home if we decide to do that; five, for me living the life my mother fell in love with and obviously continuing the search for my father..." She paused poignantly. "Someday, he will perhaps return to Corfu. If he doesn't, then we'll search the four corners of the earth until we find him."

"What about your friends? You will miss them and they'll miss you," Jake reminded her.

Rodi shrugged. "I will miss them, but Lisa is getting married next year so we'll be a ready-made honeymoon destination for her and Damien. No doubt we'll be inundated with UK visitors every summer, but I'll enjoy that!" She looked at him with a glint in her eye. "You'll love my friends and I'll love yours. Think about the free holiday accommodation we'll supply for Jonathan, Trisha and the twins. Would your parents come too, do you think?"

"I'm sure they would, but I insist we keep on working. Our capitals will earn money for us, but we don't want to touch it. That has to be for our future," Jake said.

"Agreed," Rodi stated firmly. "We are far too young to retire. I think I'd go stark raving bonkers if I wasn't working. But don't avoid the main issue here, Jake Saunders. I need to sell this house; I need to be in Corfu; I need to find my father; I need to be with you, the man I love desperately."

"Okay, okay," Jake said with a smile. "I'm convinced. We'll see the estate agent in the morning and set the ball rolling, then we'll compose your letter to the immigration office in Nicosia."

Twelve

Summer 1959
Paleocastrista, Corfu

"Do you have your passports, ladies?" the receptionist asked in impeccable English. She smiled at him and her friend nudged her grinning.

"What?" the girl enquired.

"Tell you later," her friend whispered and then she asked the receptionist, "Will you please keep our passports in the safe?"

He nodded. "Certainly, madam. Your room is four-two-five, twin room with en suite and sea view. Enjoy your holiday."

He smiled at the comments made by the more confident of the two girls and as he watched them drag their suitcases towards the elevator, the young man's heart skipped a beat. His thoughts confused him. *Cory,* he chastised himself. *You welcome pretty girls to the hotel all the time. Why is your heart thumping in your chest?* He took a deep breath to compose himself and concentrated on the next coach load of visitors who were jostling around the desk, eager to be checked in so that their holidays might begin.

A few days later, on his night off, he decided he would approach the young lady and ask her out. He checked the register to make sure he had her name correct. *Adele Bartlett*. He caught sight of her coming up from the beach. Holding himself confidently straight, he began to march in her direction. *Stop this, Cory,* he thought, feeling stupidly embarrassed at his upright stance and regimental bearing. *Be casual: smile; walk confidently, but don't make yourself look like a bumbling teenager*. "Hello," he greeted her. "How are you?"

Adele appeared to be surprised. He noticed that she twirled a strand of her hair to hide her embarrassment and he loved her for it. "Would you like to come to the Club Tropicana for dinner tonight? I would like to show you a little bit of Greek culture. I think you will enjoy it."

Adele smiled nervously. "Do you mind if I think about it?" she asked. "I'm not sure what Eva has planned for tonight, but I'll get back to you later if that's all right with you."

"That's fine by me," he said. "I am on the reception desk until four o'clock this afternoon. I do hope you'll be able to come out with me."

Adele smiled, the most disarming smile he had ever encountered. "I'll let you know as soon as I've spoken with Eva." She smiled again and went off to find her friend.

~ * ~

They had dinner whilst being entertained by Greek dancers and she laughed as the traditional smashing of plates was going on all around her. Cory was totally fascinated by his companion. "Adele, you should come to Corfu more often. I think you would like our Greek way of life."

"It sounds idyllic," she told him.

"Idyllic?" he asked. "My English vocabulary does not contain that word. What does it mean?"

She smiled. "Perfect...beautiful..."

"Like you?" he interrupted, but he noticed her cheeks flush and felt he had made her uncomfortable. "I'm sorry, Adele," he apologised. "I did not mean to embarrass you, but I like you."

She looked up shyly. "I like you too." When he heard those words, his heart somersaulted once again. His thoughts brought him down to earth. *I like this girl so much as I have never liked before. I am confused. I must do what is right...* "Shall I take you home now?" he suggested. "It's almost midnight and I ought not to keep you out so late."

Adele laughed. "While I'm in Corfu, I can stay up as long as I like," she told him. "No parents to come looking for me."

"But I must do what is right," he replied. "You are sixteen; I am twenty-one...how do you say? *In loco parentis.*"

"Please don't say that," she pleaded. "I'm responsible enough to do the right thing."

"I know that," Cory continued. "I have been watching how you talk to those English boys."

"Scottish," Adele corrected.

He shrugged. "... Scottish then, but I like the way you are friends without allowing them to be...how do you say...*oikeíos*...intimate."

Adele tapped his arm playfully. "Now you are flirting with me," she told him amicably. "I just do friendship; no need for more."

"I understand," he said. "I won't spoil it."

He dared to hold her hand as they strolled back to the hotel. The lights from several hotels along the beach were reflected in the dark blue waters of the Ionian Sea making the atmosphere magical, romantic. "May I see you again?" he asked as they arrived back at the hotel.

"I would like that," she told him.

"Unfortunately, I work during the day, but I see you in the evening. Is that all right?" he asked tentatively. "I might not be able to talk much when I work, because the manager, he does not like us to be too friendly with guests."

"Oh, well if it will get you into trouble," Adele told him, "I'll understand if you can't see me again—on a date I mean." She flushed and Cory was aware he'd made her feel awkward.

"I won't get into trouble," he said. "I'll make sure the manager he does not know I like you." He smiled. "I'll meet you by the swimming pool tomorrow night at eight o'clock. Goodnight, Adele." He kissed her on the cheek and walked away, looking back to wave and blow another kiss before he turned the corner to go to his quarters.

It was after their third date. They wandered along the steep pathway towards the beach. He held her hand as he helped her down the rugged steps and he thrilled at her touch. There was a closeness between them that night he had never experienced. His thoughts were forcing him to tread very carefully. *I do not wish to offend, Adele. Sweet, lovely Adele. In all my life I have never felt this way. It is madness. I have taken guests out before, but I have never felt like this.* He drew her close as they stepped onto the soft sand still warm from the day's sun. Their bodies came together as he gently cupped her face in his hands. Slowly, he lowered his lips to hers and they kissed passionately for the first time. "Adele; Adele," he whispered. "I have wanted to kiss you since the day I first saw you."

Adele came in close to him. He could feel her heart beating fast and he held her gently as she trembled at his touch. "I feel like I'm in another world, Cory. What is happening to me?"

He kissed her again with longing and urgency. "I love you, Adele…" He heard her catch her breath.

"I bet you say that to all the girls," she said shyly.

He held her at arms' length as he said with more than a little assertiveness, "No, no, I do not, I promise you."

He noticed the tears glisten on her cheeks and he wipe them away with caring hands. "I think I love you too, Cory," she whispered in his ear. "I have never felt like this and I don't want it to stop, but I leave the day after tomorrow and I will never see you again."

"If we are in love, love will find a way to keep us together," he told her gently. "Come, we will go back to the hotel to find your friends."

Adele held him back. "No, not yet," she said quietly. "I would like to go with you to your quarters."

Cory was surprised by her suggestion. "Adele, you don't have to do this," he told her.

"Yes, I do," she said emphatically.

"Are you sure?" he asked, trying desperately not to gather her up in his arms right there on the spot.

"I have never been so sure of anything in my life."

The following night, Adele's last night in Corfu, they dined at the local *taverna*, strolled along the beach and found a secluded spot away from the eyes of the world where they made love again under the stars. Afterwards, they clung to each other as though neither ever wanted to let go. Cory was the first to break the silence. "I love you, my sweet, beautiful Adele," he said. "I need your address so I can write to you and we can plan for our future."

"I'll write to you first and then you can reply," she suggested. "I promise I won't leave it too long when I arrive home. I shall miss you, but there is so much to consider before we can look to the future. Let's take it one step at a time."

"I shall miss you too," he said. "I know all this is my heart talking, not my head." He smiled at the girl with whom he had fallen madly and hopelessly in love.

"But once we leave, there will be lots of other guests here to take our place," she reminded him. "Tomorrow when I leave the hotel, I'll just be a memory for you."

Cory sat up and looked into her sad eyes. "Adele, Adele, Adele," he whispered. "How can I make you understand that I have never felt like this? I have told you; I have made love to you against all my previous vows never to make love to a girl only if I love her with all my heart."

"I said that too," she informed him. "I knew I was breaking my promise to myself last night, but I am so sure this is love. Don't ask me how I know in such a short time, but I do know and I have absolutely no regrets. I doubt if anybody would believe that you can fall in love so quickly."

"I fell in love at first sight," he told her. "The moment you smiled at me at the reception desk when you arrived and your friend, Eva, nudged you, I knew then. Please don't go home and forget all about me."

"I'll never do that," she assured him.

They kissed passionately for the last time and he said, "Goodnight, my darling Adele. Safe journey home and write to me soon."

Cory was working when the girls left the hotel on their way home. He waved and discreetly blew a kiss from behind the reception desk under the steely eyes of the hotel manager. He turned away as the girls went through the door and climbed into the coach that would take them to the airport and their flight back home. His thoughts were sad. *Goodbye, my dearest Adele.*

You bewitched me with your love. You stole my heart and I don't think I shall ever be the same again.

~ * ~

He waited and waited to hear from Adele, but nothing came. By the end of the holiday season, he decided that the love of his life had disappeared forever. *She promised,* he thought sadly. *Maybe she wrote and I didn't receive it. Corfiot post is not reliable, but I have no address to write to her.* Then out of the blue, his father appeared from the hotel kitchen waving a postcard.

"What is this, my boy?" he said. "Chef said it was stuck between some of the outstanding bills for supplies."

Cory couldn't understand why he was so angry, but his father was enraged. "What is wrong, *bampás*? Why are you so mad?"

His father threw the postcard towards him, but it floated onto the floor. As Cory bent to pick it up, his father put his foot on it. "You get yourself mixed up with an English girl?" he asked. "Fool! Big fool!"

"What are you talking about?" Cory asked. "Is the postcard from her?"

His father moved his foot and allowed his son to read what was written on the card... *Hello, Cory. I miss you so much. I am so busy at college at the moment, but I will write a letter soon when I have sorted out my classes. Still, here is my address.* Cory looked at the date on the postcard. "September first? How long have you had this? It's November nineteenth today. The season has finished and I've been waiting to hear from Adele since she left at the end of August."

His father glared at him and shook his head. "Stay away from women. They are no good. Look at me and learn from it..."

"Have you been drinking?" Cory asked.

"Indeed I have," was the swift reply. "I need to drink to cope with my life when I go home from work."

"What are you saying, *bampás*?" Cory was full of questions. "What has been happening while I have been living in the hotel? Are you and *màna* fighting? Is this why you are so angry with me? What did I do wrong?"

His father breathed deeply in order to compose himself. "I'm not angry with you, *gios*. I have a very unhappy life at home just now."

"Can I do anything to help?" Cory asked, conscious of the fact he was asking questions and not receiving answers.

"Sorry, *gios*; sorry. I'm going home now to face the music." He laughed sardonically. "No sweet music these days in Lakones."

"Shall I come with you?"

"No, my boy. Never let it be said that Petros Demetriou cannot sort out his own problems."

Cory patted his father on the back. "Now you sound more like the dad I know and love," he said with a smile. "You know where I am if you need me." He looked at the card in his hand and smiled again, this time at the thought that now he could write to his beloved Adele.

Back in his room, Cory wrote what was in his heart: *Hello my sweet Adele. I have waited so long to hear from you. Your postcard was lost among kitchen invoices and I have only just received it. I am so pleased to hear from you...*

As soon as he'd finished writing, he put in a copy of the photograph Eva had taken of Adele and him on the last day and posted it immediately.

Thirteen

The night he'd had the strange conversation with his father, he went to bed early. At just after midnight, there was a loud knocking on his door. "Cory! Cory! Wake up!" The security man, Arvanitis, who watched the desk during the night in the closed season sounded panic-stricken.

Sleepily, Cory ambled to the door and unlocked it. "What is it?" he asked. "Is there a fire?"

"Get dressed and come quickly," the man instructed. "It's your father."

Cory was spurred into action. "My father? What about him?"

"Just come quickly to reception when you're dressed," Arvanitis instructed. "Yannis Papakostas is waiting for you."

Cory threw on his jeans and a sweater and rushed to the reception desk. Papakostas was indeed waiting for him and as he ran towards him, he noticed tears in the eyes of his father's long-time neighbour. "What is it, Yannis? What's wrong?"

"An accident," he said. "A terrible accident."

~ * ~

The death of his father shocked the young man to the core. The news that his mother and sister had left without a trace added greatly to his heartache. All their clothes and belongings had gone so they had obviously left of their own free will. There was no note, no message, nothing. "Have you no idea where they went?" he asked the neighbours.

"We haven't spoken to any of them for weeks," Mrs Papakostas said. "All we hear is loud voices and arguing. We don't like to interfere. We are so sorry, Cory, for your loss and for your distress. If there is anything we can do..."

"There's really nothing, thank you. Even the local constabulary knows nothing except that my father was drunk and was shouting in the streets of Lakones. That poor driver." Cory shivered involuntarily. "He must be having nightmares almost as bad as mine."

With the funeral of his father over, Cory was left completely distraught and bereft. He lay in his bed at night unable to sleep. *Please God help me,* he prayed over and over again. He wept into his pillow and restlessly tossed and turned, but sleep evaded him. *Look at yourself,* he silently rebuked himself. *You are praying to a god you hardly know, a god Antonis pleaded with you to embrace. How can you expect that god to be with you in your hour of need? You flatly refused to follow his good grace. Antonis begged you and you wouldn't listen. Would you be in this psychological mess if you'd taken your friend's lead?* He sighed deeply as his mind wandered to Adele. *Sweet, beautiful Adele. You stole my heart and I so want to be with you just now. I need to feel the closeness of your love; to hear the beating of your heart in unison with mine. How can one week in your arms leave me yearning for more? Oh, not the sex, but simply the warmth of your love.*

Night after night he went over the same things in his mind. He waited for Adele to reply to his letters and then the unbelievable happened. All the letters were returned unopened—*No longer at this address. Return to sender.*

~ * ~

A week on retreat at Dionysiou with Antonis gave Cory the will to face what life might have in store for him. Although he felt completely alone, his thoughts were positive. *I need to further my studies to gain better qualifications. That way I will be able to get a better position. I'll go to Athens away from Lakones, away from Corfu. Maybe sometime I shall feel better able to cope with all that Corfu represents at the moment—so many bad memories—Dad, Mum and Ariadnê.* He sighed deeply. *Adele, my sweet Adele. My heart still yearns for you, but I fear you have gone from my life forever.*

~ * ~

In January nineteen sixty, Cory Demetriou enrolled at the School of Arts in Athens where there was a new course in hotel management. Along with fifteen other students, he embarked on his future, one of sixteen pioneers in the new world of Greek education where vocational training was on offer to a select group of students.

"Hi, I'm Tia." The girl next to him in his first lecture introduced herself.

"Cory," he replied without ceremony.

"This is so exciting, isn't it?" Tia went on. "I am so pleased to start this course, aren't you?"

Cory took a deep breath. "I'm sorry if I appear rude," he apologised, "but I am not good company at the moment. Maybe I'll talk to you later." He smiled, but he knew his heart was not behind the smile.

Tia shrugged. "That's all right," she said amicably. "I understand." She organised her books and settled back in her seat to wait for the tutor to appear.

After the lecture, in which they were all made aware of the hygiene required in kitchens and of the regulations that were required in kitchen management, Cory went for lunch and was joined by another young man on the course. The girls, only four of them, sat together at the opposite side of the refectory, chatting noisily and making sure they would all be firm friends by the end of the day. Cory's lunch-mate was Alexei, a quietly confident young man who had travelled from Rhodes to be on the course.

"Are you usually so quiet?" he asked Cory, who was displaying uncharacteristic signs of being unsociable.

Jolted out of his surly mood, Cory managed to smile. "No, I'm not," he informed the inquisitive Alexei. "Sorry, but I've had a lot on my mind recently. My father died…"

"I'm sorry."

"Thank you. All this is new to me. I haven't been in school since I was sixteen. I have worked in a hotel for the past five years, but the death of my father prompted me to try to make something more of my life. I need to spread my wings and travel a bit once I've completed this course." Cory was feeling better already. *I need to talk about things,* he thought pragmatically. *But only on my terms. Mum and Ariadnê can wait. Adele must be forever in my past.* "I'm really looking forward to the course. Maybe I will own a hotel eventually."

"Good man," Alexei said enthusiastically. "Maybe I'll join you." He paused and glanced over to where the girls were sitting. "That girl Tia keeps looking in your direction. Are you interested? I wouldn't mind spending some time with her. She's gorgeous."

Cory turned round and Tia waved coyly. He nodded, just once and slowly forcing a half-smile. Turning back to face Alexei, he said, "Not really. I have no time for girls if I am to do well on this course. My aim is to leave with honours if I'm up to it."

Alexei grinned. "Tall order when the only four girls on the course are ours for the asking," he said. "They are all lovely. Helens of Troy, all of them!"

Cory had to agree. "Yes they are, but I'm not looking for distractions."

"Give us a few weeks in their company and we'll see what you think then," Alexei said. "Do you have a girlfriend in Corfu?"

"No, not now," he admitted sadly.

Alexei said nothing. His whole demeanour manifested his astute understanding of his new friend and so he chose not to comment.

As the weeks and months went by, both young men studied hard and became friends with the other students on the course. Alexei openly wooed Tia and Leandra and eventually it was Leandra who succumbed to his charms. Tia only had eyes for Cory. The other two girls, Phedra and Stefania, had boyfriends on another course so their free time was spent off campus. By the end of the first year, Alexei, Leandra, Tia and Cory could usually be found together in the library or in a local bar. Cory still remained alone.

"When are you going to ask Tia out on a date, Cory?" Alexei enquired as they went back to the apartment they shared inside the college grounds.

"I'm not sure I will," Cory told him.

"Don't you like her?"

Cory sighed. "Yes, I do like her. She's a nice girl and I value her friendship, but I don't want the romantic entanglement. Been there, done that and when it falls apart, the heartache is unbearable. I am only just over my last..." He paused as he thought. *Was it a relationship? Was it a love affair? I thought it was real love...* "...my last girlfriend."

Alexei patted him on the back gently. "I've been hurt too, but how will you know if you can love again if you don't give it a try?"

"Not yet, Alexei. Not yet," he said quietly.

The end of semester party went with a swing. Wine and ouzo flowed and all the students let down their hair after a term of very hard work. Cory and Tia danced the night away while Alexei and Leandra declared their undying love for each other. At the end of the evening, Cory walked Tia back to her room. He placed a protective hand round her shoulders and they chatted happily, fuelled with rather more ouzos than usual.

Arriving at her door, he bent to kiss her cheek and say goodnight. *This is what friends do,* he thought. He was happy and he felt relaxed. Heads came close. They felt each other's breath on their faces. Lips came together and Tia guided him through her door.

"We shouldn't be doing this," he said, desire stirring in his loins.

"There's no rule that says we shouldn't," she replied as they began to tear at each other's clothes.

At the moment of highest passion, Cory cried out with longing and desire. "Adele! My darling Adele!"

~ * ~

During the holidays, Cory and his friends obtained positions in hotels in various parts of Greece so that they might put their newly learned skills to the test. Cory found Kings Hotel in Corinth that stayed open throughout the year. Many of the hotels closed for the winter months, or only kept on a skeleton staff from November until May. The hotel was situated on the beach a few kilometres south of the Corinth Canal, a busy thoroughfare for ocean going liners and a spectacular tourist attraction all year round. Cory shadowed the *sous chef* and gained valuable experience. During his time off, he wandered around Loutraki, chatted to locals and took pleasure in being alone.

After four weeks of work placement, he returned to Athens. Alexei was still with Leandra, but Tia was nowhere to be seen.

Fourteen

He spent three years diligently working towards his ultimate goal—qualifying with an honours degree in hotel management. Tia had reportedly undertaken a course in sociology and cut all ties with the hotel management group. Cory felt guilty.

"I could say I don't remember what happened that night," he told Alexei, "but I would be lying. I betrayed Tia and I disgraced myself. I accept that."

"Oh don't be so dramatic, Cory," Alexei said light-heartedly. "You are not the first person to get your leg over and call out a past lover's name and you won't be the last. Tia told Leandra what happened."

"Oh saints preserve us!" Cory exclaimed. "I'm ashamed I did that to Tia. I meant her no harm. The drink and the heat of the moment just led us to that place. I hate to think I ruined Tia's ambitions."

"Stop beating yourself up about it," Alexei told him. "Tia was going to leave hotel management anyway. She decided quite early in the course that it wasn't what she wanted to do. She deliberated long and hard about it and Leandra persuaded her to do the first year and then decide where her ambition was leading."

Cory breathed a sigh of relief. "I can't say I'm proud of what I did, but I'm pleased I wasn't the sole reason for Tia's change of mind."

"Don't flatter yourself, Demetriou," his close friend interrupted. "Lovely Tia is already seeing an engineer from Athens University so you didn't break her heart after all!"

"That's the end of that then," Cory said. "I wish I had your devil-may-care attitude sometimes, but now I can aim for my honours degree and please don't lead me into any more temptation, Mr Matthias."

Alexei shook his hand. "Hang on in there, Cory. Some day you will find love again."

~ * ~

The next few years were kind to Cory. He gained the honours he had worked for and accepted the position of under-manager at Hotel Electra in Athens just a stone's throw away from the college. He loved Athens and Athens had been good to him. After the perfect grounding in all aspects of hotel management, he secured a position as hotel manager in Protaras, Cyprus.

Nineteen seventy in Cyprus was not the calmest of times. The UN peacekeeping forces had been ensconced since nineteen sixty-four, but there was underlying unrest and Cory felt it.

"Is this the reason for your departure?" he asked the outgoing manager as he indicated the military presence outside the hotel.

Dion Vasiliou shook his head. "Not at all," he replied. "We Greeks are confident that Cyprus is in safe hands. I'm leaving because I am migrating to America. My family is there already. My children will grow up in the land of the free and the home of the brave."

"Sounds wonderful," Cory said almost enviably. "I see I am taking over a well-run hotel. Thank you."

"Everything is in good order. The staff are well trained and know the ropes. We open for nine months of the year, but you already know that. Your telephone interview was the best we have ever experienced. You certainly know what you are doing."

"Thank you. I try to do my best," Cory answered. "I am looking forward to my time here."

Vasiliou left three days later and Cory settled in very quickly. Hotel Mediterranean reminded him of Hotel Helenya and he was very comfortable there. Ghosts of the past no longer troubled him and he determined he would grow as a manager and as a person in these surrounds.

~ * ~

For four years he welcomed thousands of guests and instigated sweeping changes in the way the popular hotel functioned. He introduced an entertainments programme which incorporated professional artistes flown in every weekend from the UK. Most were just on the brink of their professional careers and the tourists who were mostly British, loved them. In addition, he employed children's reps who were qualified to supervise children during the day and keep them occupied with holiday activities while parents relaxed. Hotel Mediterranean set the pace for the whole of northeast Cyprus.

"Don't you ever rest?" Irena asked him.

"Of course," he replied. "Why do you ask?"

Irena was a receptionist, not the youngest of his staff, far from it. "I have worked for you for four years and I have never seen you take a day off," she told him. "I know you make a point of not socialising with your staff, but why don't you join my husband and me tonight for dinner at Hellas Taverna? It will do you good."

Cory sighed. *Apart from business lunches and dinners, I haven't been out for ages. I ought to accept. I have no reason not to. What harm can it do and her husband will be there.* "You know,' he said with a smile. "I'd love to. It will make a pleasant change. I've almost forgotten what it's like to go out for dinner."

"Good," Irena said as she amicably tapped him on the arm. "We'll see you at eight o'clock."

"Fine," he replied. "That will give me time to see dinner well on the way here."

Irena laughed. "Chef is more than capable of making sure dinner runs smoothly here. Just relax and delegate for a change."

Cory smiled. He liked this lady and she was only looking out for him in a motherly kind of way. "All right, *mana,*" he said to the matronly figure before him. "I'll be there at eight. Thank you."

He discovered he was joining the whole family for dinner, not just Irena and her husband. "This is my husband, Nik and these are our children and their partners—Adelphos, our eldest and Stella, Pierro and Talia, Jason and Leah and this is our youngest, Melinda."

Cory nodded to each in turn inwardly panicking. *Lovely people, but...Melinda has no partner. Surely Irena wouldn't set me up... Please God, no!*

Dinner was good; the company was great. "Thank you for inviting me," he said as he prepared to leave. "Please allow me to pay the bill. I appreciate the night out. It is such a long time since..."

"...Since you relaxed." Irena completed his sentence for him.

"We can't allow you to pay for us all," Nik told him. "If you insist, let's go halves. I'd be happy with that."

"Right. We'll do that if you have no objections," Cory agreed. "Can we all walk home together? We all live in the same direction, don't we?"

"All except me. I turn off before we get to Hotel Mediterranean," Melinda said. She had been very quiet all evening, Cory noticed, surly almost and he considered she was different to the rest of her family.

"Oh well, I'll walk home with you if you like," he suggested.

"No it's all right," she said. "I am used to walking back by myself. It's only a stone's throw from my parents' house."

Irena intervened. "Mr Demetriou has made a kind offer, Melinda," she told her daughter. "Just be sociable for once and allow him to walk back to your apartment. It's on his way back to the hotel anyway."

Melinda looked at Cory. "Thank you," she said politely. "I appreciate your kindness."

The rest of the family dropped off couple by couple until there was just Melinda and Cory left. He stuffed his hands in his pockets so as not to feel awkward. She did the same.

"What do you do?" he asked, "When you are not with your family, I mean."

"I'm a student."

"That's interesting. What are you studying?" Cory was genuinely interested in those who made the most of their education.

"I am studying history, politics and economics," she informed him with a certain bitterness in her tone. "I have returned to university after working in Nicosia. Living there opens your eyes to what is happening in Cyprus at the moment."

"You sound angry," Cory said quietly. "How long were you in Nicosia? You are still quite young."

"Not too young to know that there's unrest amongst the greater population of our island," she objected. "I was there for five years, long enough to listen to whispers in bars and cafes. Are you aware that the Greek nationalists are planning a *coup d'état* that will incite Turkey to attack? Do you even care?"

"My goodness, Melinda, you are seriously angry about it, aren't you?' Cory said, not hiding his dismay.

"We're here," she interrupted. "This is where I live. Thank you for walking home with me. Good night." And she went inside without another word.

She is one seriously intense young woman, he thought as he wandered back to the hotel. *So unlike the rest of her family.*

~ * ~

The following week he decided to drive to Famagusta. He had known since he first arrived in Cyprus that it had been transformed from an old Turkish town into a modern harbour city. He had thought many times he would go and see for himself, but typically when things are on one's doorstep, one doesn't make the effort. Famagusta was apparently flourishing, but many Greeks had already packed up and left, thinking they might return when the feeling of unrest had disappeared. His decision to go on that day, August fourteen, nineteen seventy-four, was ill-advised. As he drove into the south of the town, he suddenly came upon Turkish tanks and he heard the deafening sound of aircraft overhead. As he attempted to turn around and flee from the attack, a Turkish bomb dropped and completely wiped out the road behind him. His escape route was totally obliterated. He was trapped.

Fifteen

Dear Miss Bartlett,

We have received your letter of the 15th January and need to inform you that we need proof of identification before we might proceed with your enquiry. Certified copies of your birth certificate and any proof that you are related to the person for whom you are searching must be forwarded to us forthwith.

Yours sincerely,

"What?" Rodi cried as she read the communication. "It's taken them six weeks to ask me for identification? What a load of contentious nonsense. How the hell am I supposed to provide all this stuff? It's back to square one again. I can't bloody well prove who I am. I already told them that!"

"Rodi," Jake said gently in order to pacify her. "Don't fly off the handle. We'll work it out. The hotel has a photocopier and we'll find a lawyer who will certify the copies for us."

"What copies?" she questioned angrily. "My father's name isn't on my birth certificate. Are they going to accept my mother's will as proof? All this red tape..."

"Calm down," Jake instructed. "We can only do as they ask, but we'll plead our case and hope they will show some compassion."

"Compassion?" she asked, the irritation still evident in her tone. "I need understanding and acknowledgement that I'm speaking the truth. Is that too much to ask?"

"*We* know you are speaking the truth, but they don't know you from Adam," Jake told her. "Anybody could ask for private information about Cory Demetriou, even somebody with a grudge. They're not going to hand out information willy-nilly."

Rodi sighed. "I get so frustrated, darling. It's not fair, it just isn't fair." Her voice faltered as she fought back the tears.

Jake took her in his arms and held her tightly. He nuzzled her hair and whispered, "We'll find him sometime, baby. I feel it in my bones." He looked into her eyes. "We have to go to work now, sweetheart. Our first coach-load of guests arrives this afternoon. We have to earn some money before we can take off on our travels again, that is *if* we have to travel again.

"I'm not totally convinced Demetriou will still be in Cyprus. The past few years have been pretty dire over there. Even now Greece and Turkey have not settled their differences. It's a divided country and still an unstable situation. If he went there in nineteen seventy as we have been led to believe, he would have been right in the conflict, assuming he stayed four or five years as he did with his previous job. Still, we have all season to work out our next move. Maybe by October, we shall have convinced the Cypriot immigration office we are genuine in our endeavours."

"I know you're right, darling," she agreed. "I'm so looking forward to work again and Eva will be here in August. She makes me feel close to Mum and in a peculiar way, close to my father too. Fate smiled upon me the day I met her and Jean-Paul."

~ * ~

"Look at you!" Eva exclaimed when she saw how well Rodi was looking. "And what is that on your finger?"

"Jake proposed to me on Christmas Day," Rodi told her, holding out her left hand to show Eva her ring."

"And you didn't tell me on the phone!" Eva exclaimed.

Rodi looked sheepish. "We hadn't told Jake's parents when I spoke to you," she explained, "and since then we have made lots of decisions about our future."

Eva gave her a hug. "Congratulations, darling. I am so happy for you. When are you getting married?"

Rodi smiled. "When I find my father," she stated.

Eva gaped. "But that might take forever, Rodi," she said wide-eyed.

"I know, but I won't wait until we're old and grey," she said with a smile. "Jake and I are happy with our lot at the moment, and actually, we are coming to live in Corfu permanently."

"Wow!" Eva exclaimed. "I can well understand that, seeing Corfu is in your blood and in your heart. Good luck to you both."

"Thank you, Eva." Rodi paused significantly. "Will you come to my wedding when it happens? I'd love it if you could stand in for Mum."

Eva couldn't speak. She nodded and allowed the tears to flow unashamedly.

~ * ~

The day Eva and Jean-Paul left, Rodi received a call from the estate agent in Worthing to say the house had been sold. "That's fantastic," she enthused. "What do I have to do now?"

"You need to sign the documents then we can exchange contracts," she was told. "I'll post them."

Rodi was quick to interrupt. "Oh no, please don't mail anything. It might take weeks to get here."

"Well what do you suggest I do?" the estate agent asked. "I could fax the documents to you if you have a fax machine."

Rodi sighed. "The hotel where I work has a fax machine, but I would prefer not to allow them to see my business transactions."

"Your solicitor is already drawing up the draft contract. Do you wish to leave the house on the market in case the sale falls through?"

"Am I allowed to do that?" Rodi asked. "How serious are the buyers?"

"Very serious, and they are first time buyers so no chain, but in your own interest, leave it on the market until contracts are exchanged."

Rodi agreed. "I think I might have an idea," she said. "My close friend and her husband are coming out here next week. I could ask her to pick up the documents and bring them with her. I'll sign them and she will return them to the solicitor when she returns to the UK. She'll be here for two weeks, but it will still be quicker than the postal service to and from Corfu."

Her friends, Lisa and Damien, arrived at the beginning of September, newly wed and very happy to see Rodi and Jake. "I so wanted you at the wedding, Rodi," Lisa told her, "but I did understand that you weren't able to fly back to England in the middle of the holiday season. Perhaps we should have married in the winter so you could have been there."

"Sorry, Lisa," Rodi said apologetically. "I would have loved to have been there, but there is no way we could leave at this time of the year. Still, you look great and I can't wait to see the photos."

"You'll be the first to get copies and I insist we have pride of place on your coffee table until you and Jake are married. Then your photo will take over," Lisa told her. "Now we have some papers from your solicitor to give to you."

"Oh yes," Rodi said, "but they can be signed later. We have two weeks together although Jake and I will have to leave you to your own devices during the day and on some evenings, but I don't think you'll be short of things to do. You are on honeymoon after all!" She took the envelope from Lisa and placed it on the bookcase until she found the time to go through the papers and sign them before Lisa and Damien left.

"I can't believe the time has gone by so quickly," she told Lisa on the night before she and Damien were due to leave. "I have so loved you being here. I'll miss you when you leave."

"I'll miss you too, Rodi. The old homestead won't be the same without you," Lisa said. "And, my dear friend, you'd better sign those papers now otherwise the house sale won't go through."

Rodi picked up the envelope from the bookshelf. She hadn't touched it since Lisa had given it to her two weeks before. "Oh dear," she said guiltily. "I hope they aren't too complicated for me to understand."

"They're not," Lisa assured her.

"And how would you know, Mrs Wilson?" she asked with a grin. "Are you an expert in property conveyancing all of a sudden?"

"No, but Damien and I bought a house just before we came out here. We don't want to be renting our apartment forever," Lisa explained.

Rodi read through the documents. As she found the page where she had to sign, her jaw dropped. "You sneaky person, Lisa Wilson!" she exclaimed.

Damien and Jake joined them when they heard the shrieks coming from the living room.

"Did you know about this, Jake Saunders?" she questioned.

Jake nodded.

"So why didn't you tell me?" she asked and then more menacing, "Why didn't you all tell me?"

"And spoil the surprise?" Jake said. "Nothing would have made me miss seeing the look on your face a couple of minutes ago. It was priceless."

Hugs all round and sincere thanks from Rodi to her dear friends, created a most wonderful last night for them all. "This is a night I'll remember for the rest of my life," Rodi told them. "Thank you for making my move from Worthing so easy. Knowing you will be living in the home where I grew up gives me so much pleasure. Now, your children can be raised in a loving family home that was made for them. Good luck and may all your problems be little ones!"

Sixteen

Rodi looked at the postmark on the envelope for a long time before she found the courage to open it.

Nicosia
11 October 1982
Dear Miss Bartlett,

We are in receipt of certified copies of your birth certificate, your United Kingdom passport and of your mother, Adele Bartlett's will. It is not possible for us to supply information without legal proof of relationship to a citizen of Greece, but we understand the nature of your enquiry. Taking into consideration that the identity of the person you claim is your father cannot be proven, personal details of that person may not be disclosed.

She sat down and handed the letter to Jake. "Damn and blast the Cypriots," she declared acidly. "I somehow had a feeling this might happen. The gist of the previous communication from them more or less warned me."

Jake took her hand. "What can I say, sweetheart?" he asked. "I'm as disappointed as you are, but we'll just have to re-think our plans."

"All our research so far is up the Swanee, she said despairingly. "I don't know what else we can do. We traced him to Cyprus, but now we don't know whether he was there or not."

"Reading between the lines," Jake said, "I think he definitely was there. They actually said they cannot disclose personal information which to me means they have that information on file, but are unable to let you have it."

"Do you think we should go to Protaras?" she asked without the previous enthusiasm she had shown earlier in the search.

"I don't know," Jake told her. "Let's sleep on it and work out what we should do in a couple of days. In the meantime, we have some work to do before we can take our winter leave and some intense negotiation with the real estate guy if we are to buy the house overlooking the bay in Paleocastritsa. We don't want to miss out on that view."

"No, we don't," Rodi agreed, "but we'll have to change those pink walls! Why would anybody want a bright pink house? Five bedrooms all with en suite will be perfect. We could open our own hotel!"

"I don't think so, darling. Those bedrooms are for our family and friends, not to mention our children."

"Hold on, Mr Saunders. Too many things on the agenda before then," she said laughing.

"Well, at least I got you smiling again," Jake said as he hugged her and kissed her cheek. "Come on, Hotel Helenya needs us."

~ * ~

Moving into the house put the search on hold. The pink villa was transformed into the white house and most of Rodi's furniture was transported by container ship to Corfu and then along the dusty roads to their new home. By the beginning of December, everything was in place including new furniture for the master suite and a new kitchen with all the latest integrated appliances.

"We'll spend a wonderful Christmas in our first home together," Rodi announced at breakfast on the first day of their winter break.

"We'll enjoy that," Jake agreed. "I can't believe how much has happened since last Christmas. At least this year we don't have to go north to visit my parents!"

"Will they be sad that we're not in England for Christmas?" she asked.

"I don't think so," he said. "They're used to me being away. Even before I met you, I didn't always go home for Christmas. Usually one of the team invited me to stay and for a time, that was preferable to Mum trying to set me up with most of the available girls in Rivington." He paused, coughed deliberately and then continued. "That is, all the available *nice* girls in Rivington. Mum's choice and mine never matched...until now." He winked at the young woman who had made him happier than he had ever been.

"Thanks, babe," she said and blew him a kiss across the breakfast table.

"All thanks should go to you for applying for a job on my team," he said with a grin, "but I'll take some of the credit for seeing your potential straight away."

Rodi laughed. "You are incorrigible…" She paused pointedly. "…but I like you!"

"Only like?" he asked with affected offence.

"Play your cards right and I might just improve on that before the day's out," she told him.

Jake shook his head slowly. "What are you like?" he asked. "But what are we going to do about the search, babe? We've been so wrapped up in the house, we haven't thought about it for a while."

Rodi rested her elbows on the table and cupped her chin in her hands. "I never stop thinking about it, Jake. I can see no way of getting further with the Cyprus information other than trying to find the hotel where he worked. I know it might sound mad, but do you think we could find a list of hotels in Protaras and simply phone them and ask? It would be cheaper and less time consuming than going there, especially if we are on a wild goose chase."

"I think that's an excellent idea," he said excitedly. "I'm not sure how we'll find a list of hotels, but we could see if Telly at the hotel will allow us to use the computer. There might be a database for Grecian Tours hotels. It's worth a try."

"That's a brilliant idea, but failing that, we can get a whole pile of holiday brochures and see what turns up for Protaras in those," she added. "Let's see what we can find before we start sorting out Christmas."

~ * ~

The hotel's computer was down and the manager didn't know when it would be fixed. "This new-fangled equipment is only as good as the person who programmed it," he said sardonically. "We still need to pick up a phone to confirm bookings. Wouldn't it be wonderful to be able to do all this paperwork just at the press of a key? Somebody needs to invent such a computer. I wish

I could do it. I wouldn't be a hotel manager anymore. I'd be a permanent guest in a penthouse suite." He laughed. "In my dreams, Jake; in my dreams."

"Do we have any Grecian Tours brochures in the hotel?" Jake asked. "We are looking for hotels in Protaras, Cyprus."

"Go to filing cabinet G and then to drawer B," he was instructed. "You'll find what we have there under C."

"Thanks, Telly."

Between them, Jake and Rodi made a list of all the Protaras hotels they could find in the brochures.

"Who's to say the hotel would be a Grecian Tours hotel anyway?" Rodi said despondently.

"We just have to take a risk on that, babe," Jake replied. "Anyway, I've written a few from Thomson's brochure and Eurotrips. We need to keep our options open. Let's have lunch at Tropicana and then go back home to start ringing round."

As they ate lunch, Rodi had a brainwave. "How long has this place been here?" she asked.

"I don't know, but we can find out. Why do you ask?" Jake noticed the excitement in Rodi's eyes.

"This is the sort of place Mum would have loved," she said. "We used to go to the English equivalent in Worthing—The Olympus Taverna. She loved Greek food." She paused significantly and grinned. "Well, she would, wouldn't she?"

When the waiter arrived with their moussaka, Jake engaged him in conversation. "Has this place been here a long time?" he asked.

"I don't know, but I'll ask chef," the waiter replied.

Rodi winked at Jake. "Your Greek is coming along well," she complimented. "The waiter didn't grimace at all when you asked the question."

The waiter returned and told them the Tropicana had been there for about twenty-five years, but the owners had changed several times since nineteen sixty.

"Is there—anybody still here—who worked in the Tropicana—then?" Jake asked falteringly.

The waiter shrugged, but offered the name of an old gentleman who came for dinner every Saturday. "Old Spiros worked as a waiter then."

"Maybe we'll come to meet him on Saturday then. Will you be working so you can introduce us?"

"Why do you want to know all this? He must be well into his sixties now, but he likes to bring his wife here every week." The waiter was curious.

"We know somebody whom we think might have come to dinner here in nineteen fifty-nine. She would have been with a Greek friend and we wondered if anybody remembered them," Jake explained.

The waiter smiled. "Come on Saturday—early, about six o'clock. Mr and Mrs Tavoularis will be here. If anybody remembers, it will be Spiros. He's like the Oracle!"

"*Efharistó*. Thank you," Jake said. We'll certainly be here."

Rodi couldn't contain her excitement. "Wow!" she exclaimed. "Just as I thought we'd come to a standstill, up pops another possibility. May be this Tavoularis guy will remember Cory, even if he doesn't remember Mum. Oh Jake!"

"Calm down, Rodi," Jake told her. "How many times do I have to remind you not to bank on things?"

"Oh, I know, babe, but I can't help it," she said, tears glistening in her eyes. "I thought I was learning to cope sensibly with any little bit of information, however small, but this has come out of the blue and it feels massive after the Cyprus setback. Just let me dream for a little while, darling...please."

Jake smiled affectionately. "How can I object to a plea like that? You are so full of wonder and hope, my baby, and I love every fibre of you because of it. Come on, let's go home and see what we might unearth with our calls to Protaras."

Armed with a long list of hotels, Jake sat with phone and systematically called and crossed off each hotel one by one. Rodi busied herself making mince pies and generally preparing for Christmas while Jake did the phoning.

Earlier she had asked him to go through the list. "Will you please call the hotels for me, darling? I don't trust my nerves and I don't want to be upset when they say they've never heard of Cory Demetriou."

Hotel after hotel, Jake received negative responses. Hotel Grecian, Protaras Bay, Hotel Narcissi, Angelique Hotel. *'I'm sorry we have no record of Cory Demetriou here.'* It was the same reply over and over again. He sighed deeply. "I think I'll stop for a while, Rodi. I need a break. Maybe I'll continue again tomorrow."

~ * ~

When Saturday came, they still had not had any positive feedback from the phone calls and Jake could do little to dispel Rodi's despair.

"I feel like giving up," she announced. "It's just too difficult."

Jake sighed. "We can't give up, baby," he said firmly. "I know you are feeling down at the moment, but we have to hang in there. We should leave it until after Christmas, though. There isn't much we can do during the festive season anyway. Many of the hotels close down. Let's go out for dinner and see if we can meet Spiros Tavoularis. He might have some information to lift our spirits."

Rodi and Jake were already in The Tropicana when the elderly couple arrived. Otis, the waiter who had spoken with them previously, signalled to Jake as they entered and went to assist them to their table next to where Rodi and Jake were sitting.

"*Kalispéra*, good evening," Jake greeted them as they took their seats and Rodi smiled warmly.

"*Kalispéra*," the old man replied. "*Ti kánete?*"

"We are well," Jake offered. "And you?"

"Good, good," Tavoularis said.

"Can we buy you and your wife a drink?" Jake asked politely. "We would like to speak with you...if you don't mind."

With the help of Otis and their combined efforts of attempting each other's language, they somehow got through the basic questions: *Have you lived in Paleocastritsa all your life? How long have you been coming here? Did you know many of the regular clientele? Did you know a young man by the name of Cory...?*

"Cory Demetriou! I did know him!" Mr Tavoularis exclaimed. "A very nice young man. He worked at Hotel Helenya."

Rodi wanted to hug him. "Tell us more," she urged.

"He used to come here with his friends from the hotel. Usually they would just have dinner and leave."

Rodi was growing more interested by the minute. "Otis, please ask him if there were any girls with him?"

"Not very often," the old man recalled. "There was usually a mixed group—boys and girls—not couples, you know. Just friends having a meal together. I remember because in those days, so many pretty girls from overseas would come in and..." He paused while he stood and demonstrated. He put his hand on his hip and looked coyly at Rodi. Winking at her, he cocked his head to one side and intimated that he wanted her to join him. They all laughed at his antics and then he became serious again. "Those Greek guys lapped up the attention, but never got involved. Too many foreign girls, you see. Better just to look, I think." He shrugged. "What fools! I would have jumped at the chance at their age!"

Mrs Tavoularis joined in the banter. "You had me at home, Spiros Tavoularis. You wouldn't dare!"

Rodi looked disappointed, but the old man continued. "I remember once, though, when Cory had a girl with him..."

"Ask him what she was like," Rodi said excitedly.

"It's such a long time ago, but it sticks in my mind because it was unusual to see any of the boys from Hotel Helenya with girls. The manager back then apparently had strict rules about fraternising with guests. I remember the manager guy. He didn't socialise much himself, so I guess he expected the same from his employees."

"Please," Rodi pleaded. "Please tell us...tell us about the girl."

"Rodi, stop interrupting," Jake advised. "You can't be sure it would be your mum."

Rodi sighed, but agreed with Jake that she should allow Tavoularis to continue.

"Cory Demetriou brought a girl in here a couple of times, a very pretty girl, very young and not unlike you," he said to Rodi. "I remember her because she seemed timid at first and then she joined in the dancing and the plate smashing. Tourists loved all that sort of thing. This place was more of a club in those days, not just a restaurant. Cory was in love and it showed."

Tears glistened in Rodi's eyes and Jake squeezed her hand to calm her.

"Soon he was alone again and he was sad. I knew he was sad, I could see it in his eyes," Tavoularis told them. "I asked him once, but he shrugged without answering. Then..." He stopped and shook his head. "Then the poor guy lost his father and after that, I never saw him again. I have no idea what happened to him after that."

Rodi allowed the tears to flow and Jake tried to comfort her. "Darling," he said gently. "We can only hope the girl was your mum, but how could we possibly know? Of course we want to think that the love Cory displayed in the restaurant was for your mum, but..."

"Have you any idea what year it would have been?" Rodi asked through her tears.

The old man was pensive. He smiled as he recalled, "It was the year my daughter was born, because that night I was called home to my wife who was in labour...yes, it was that night because Cory asked if he could help...give me a ride home...and I can give you the actual month too...August...August twenty-ninth, nineteen fifty-nine."

Rodi gasped. "That has to be Mum," she concluded and she went to hug Tavoularis. "Thank you," she said. "At least I know now that my father loved my mum and that means a lot at this point in my life. Thank you so much."

The four people dined together that night and, fuelled with several glasses of wine, Spiros reminisced some more, not to the advantage of the search, but much to the amusement of them all.

~ * ~

Christmas nineteen eighty-two came and went and Rodi and Jake heralded in the new year with renewed enthusiasm. They began the telephone calls to Cyprus again at the end of January, considering that even when the hotels weren't open for business, there would be managers and office staff there to prepare for the on-coming season. Jake took up the challenge again. Since the night with Spiros Tavoularis, Rodi had been more in control of her emotions, but she still needed Jake's calming influence and his sensible, reasonable approach when talking to faceless strangers hundreds of miles away.

The first few enquiries gained negative replies, but then he called the Hotel Mediterranean. He had methodically listed them in alphabetical order so he was more than half way down his list.

"Hotel Mediterranean, boró na sas voithíso? Can I help you?"

"Good morning," Jake said. "Can we speak in English, please?"

"Certainly, sir. How can I help you?"

"My fiancée and I are trying to locate a gentleman by the name of Cory Demetriou whom we believe managed a hotel in Protaras around the year nineteen seventy and probably after that date."

There was momentary silence at the other end of the line.

"Hello?" Jake said. He heard the person catch her breath. "Hello?" he said again.

"Just one moment, please, sir..."

Seventeen

Famagusta 1974

Cory's initial reaction was to put his foot down on the accelerator and challenge the tank that was bearing down on him. He instinctively turned the steering wheel to avoid being in the direct path of the iron monster and realised the tank would not, or could not turn to chase him if he drove past at high speed. Aircraft zoomed overhead, swooping and diving and making a deafening noise as bombs dropped all around him. He pulled over to the side of the road that was littered with rubble. He could see the crescent and star of the Turkish flag on the tank which was approaching and he wondered if he would get out of this alive.

Unrelenting, the tank came forward and changed course so as to be in direct line with the car. Cory slid down in his seat, making himself as inconspicuous as possible. The tank came nearer and nearer. Cory kept his hand on the door handle in order to open it and roll out of the car at the last second before the tank hit. Heart beating wildly in his chest, he heard the thundering of the beast as it prepared to mow him down. He flung open the door, threw himself to the ground and rolled away as his car was flattened only a couple of metres from him. Then all went black.

~ * ~

When he opened his eyes, he was sitting upright on a hard chair, his arms were tied behind him and his feet tied at the ankles. "*Ti eínai aftó?* What is this?" he murmured.

Silence.

He breathed in deeply. His ribs hurt and his head was throbbing. Looking round as best he could, he determined he was in a small room with a shuttered window to his left and a door directly in front of him. "*Voithíste me!*" he called. "Help me!"

Still no response.

He planted his fettered feet on the ground and tried to take his weight. With his arms tied firmly to the chair, he struggled to stand. Several times he managed to lean forward and inch towards the door, but his ribs were too painful and he had to stop. *How on earth did I get here?* he thought, his mind totally confused. *I remember seeing the tank coming towards me, but I don't know what happened next.*

Suddenly the door burst open and two people dressed in black from head to toe stood threateningly before him. Their faces were covered and the bigger of the two spoke. "What were you doing in Famagusta yesterday?"

Cory's head hurt, but he realised he must not intimidate his aggressors. "I think I was just visiting..."

"Think? Think?" the man shouted. "What do you mean you think?" His face was inches away from Cory's.

Feeling like a fly caught in a spider's web, Cory leaned back as far as he was able. "My head hurts…"

"That'll be the blow you gave him," the other person said and Cory was taken aback. It was a woman's voice, a voice he thought he had heard before.

"Please, may I have some air?" he gasped. "This room is stuffy and my head hurts. I can't breathe."

The big guy reacted with hostility. "Your head will hurt more if you don't give us answers," he said angrily.

"Don't hit him again," the woman instructed. "He won't be any use to us if he's unconscious." Then to Cory, "Why did you come to Famagusta yesterday of all days? The Turks had made it clear they would attack. Don't you listen to the news?"

Cory breathed in deeply again and winced. "Not the best of my decisions," he groaned. "I just intended to look around the city. I never had the chance before, or I never took the opportunity to visit previously. Nothing sinister. I didn't think the Turks were serious. Just bad judgement on my part."

"Pathetic," the big guy spat. "You sympathise with the Turks? You are traitor to Greek Cypriots? We should just kill you now so you can do no more damage to our beloved country." He leaned over Cory, his fist ready to punch him in the face.

"Stop it," the woman said. "I'm not so sure he is the man we want."

The big guy continued. "What do you know, traitor? Give us all you know."

"Stop!" the woman said again. "Our leader does not like violence…"

"He's weak," the big guy said with venom in his voice. "I should be leader; treat violence with violence. It's the only way to get answers. This guy knows something. I feel it."

"I know nothing," Cory said weakly. "I'm not a Cypriot, but I am Greek. I sympathise with your cause and would do nothing to hinder what you are doing."

"I don't believe you," his would-be attacker said threateningly.

The woman grabbed her compatriot's arm. "Leave him for now. We'll seek advice."

"Weak woman," he said scathingly. "Why our so-called illustrious leader gave you the power to issue orders, I don't know."

"Because I think before I act and speak," she informed him firmly. "Give him a drink and let's get out of here."

"Don't leave me tied up," Cory pleaded.

"As if we'd be so stupid," the guy told him.

"Untie his feet," the woman instructed. "He'll get nowhere with his arms tied to a chair." She placed a bottle of water to his lips and allowed him to drink. With no further instructions, the two left.

Just before dawn the following day, Cory heard rustling outside. Quietly the door opened and a person came in. No words were spoken and Cory's hands were untied.

"Who are you?" he asked.

"You don't need to know," she told him. "Just make your way south to the edge of the town. There will be a car waiting. Say nothing to the driver. He has instructions to drop you off in Protaras. Say nothing of this to anybody."

"Melinda? Is it you?" he asked as he rubbed his wrists to ease the discomfort.

"You don't need to know who I am," she said harshly.

"I am not a fool," he told her.

"It seems obvious that you are. Only a fool would have ventured into Famagusta two days ago."

Cory was embarrassed. "Point taken," he said, "But please be careful. Fight for your cause if you must, but don't put yourself in danger unnecessarily." He winced again as he felt his ribs and the back of his head. "Did you have to be so brutal?"

"You were clearly mistaken for a Turkish citizen, an interloper."

Cory laughed sardonically. "It seems you were a bit naïve, Melinda..."

"Who says I'm Melinda?"

"Okay, okay, but you were still naïve. Why would the Turkish tanks mow down their own man?"

"Most of the Greeks had fled. Some of those who didn't were killed in the bombing. The Turks will do anything to infiltrate our lines," she replied. "We trust nobody. Look what happened to you. Now, go before dawn breaks and don't forget, say absolutely nothing to anybody."

"How do you know you can trust me?" he asked as he left.

"I know," she said. "You are Greek."

~ * ~

The car dropped him off a couple of hundred metres from the hotel. The masked driver didn't speak and Cory followed instructions in keeping silent too. He slipped into the hotel unnoticed through the rear entrance and went to his room. After a shower and a couple of hours sleep, he felt reasonably refreshed.

"Where have you been?" Chef asked when he appeared in the kitchen. "Have you found yourself a woman?" He winked at his boss. "Two nights? Be careful, boss man," he joked. "Too much of you-know-what will sap your energy!"

Cory gave him a look of disdain. "I might have been with a woman, but not in the way you think, so watch what you say," he said, deliberately joining in with the joke to hide the fear he still felt inside.

"Lost your bottle, have you?" Chef said laughing.

"Just get on with your work, Chef. Breakfast in half an hour."

He managed to cope until the end of the season, then Cory decided to give notice and move on. He left quietly, only informing Irena where he was going. She was his long-time loyal receptionist and personal assistant, and he knew she would be discreet.

Eighteen

From Cyprus, he returned to Athens and stayed unrecognised in an apartment in the south of the city. He needed to recover from the ordeal, and he hadn't realised how much he had been running on adrenalin since his experience in Famagusta. Being alone was his way of dealing with his trauma. Everything had changed in Athens. Even the hotel where he worked had a new name and he kept away from it. Each day, he wandered along the waterfront at Piraeus. Taking in the peaceful view and watching the yachts in the marina, he gradually began to relax and enjoy his life again. His doctor had been instrumental in his recovery.

"What do you intend to do now that you don't need me anymore?" the doctor asked.

"I'd like to travel. I met somebody once who went to America. That really appeals to me," he told her. "I would like to trace my mother and my sister too. It has been so long since I saw them," he continued sadly. "It's hard to believe they haven't tried to contact me, but Corfu must have held too many bad memories for them. I have to think that I'm not one of those memories, but I know my father was the cause of their running away. I was always very close to my father, but I know he didn't make my mother's life easy."

"Does that make you as sad as you sound?" the doctor continued.

"Sad yes, but not depressed, if that's what you're hinting, doctor." He liked the doctor. She had helped him cope when he first arrived in Piraeus a year ago. "I really don't know where to start looking, but my mother often talked about going overseas. I suppose there are ways and means of finding out if she left the country."

"Your plans sound good and you certainly have the right qualifications to start up a business anywhere in the world. I often think I should go overseas too before I get too old to settle somewhere new," she said smiling. "You and I should pool our resources, so to speak, and head into the wide blue yonder."

Cory looked at her wide-eyed. "Are you propositioning me?" he asked laughing. "Because if you are, I'm interested."

"I might be," she replied, laughing too. "But I guess we should be on neutral territory before we talk personal plans."

"You are serious, aren't you?" he asked dismayed.

"I am if you are," she stated cheerily. "Let's meet for dinner and discuss our plans."

~ * ~

Doctor Jacinta Rodino and Mr Cory Demetriou met for dinner on what was meant to be a strictly platonic basis. She was thirty-one years old and he was thirty-seven. Neither of them had married; both were free spirits. They dined at the Trexantiri Fish Restaurant, overlooking the bay and the harbour.

"I am quite overwhelmed that you have given up your time to dine with me," Cory told her. "It isn't every day a doctor invites me to dinner."

"My pleasure, Cory," she said amicably. "Please call me Jacinta. We are now friends, not doctor and patient. If we are going to travel together, we need to get to know each other properly." She smiled, a warm smile that told him she was indeed his friend.

Conversation flowed easily and by the end of the evening, they felt they were no longer just acquaintances, but firm friends. They laughed and joked, discussed topics serious and frivolous, shared stories of their childhood.

"Why did you never marry, Cory?" she asked. "You're a handsome guy with a great personality. I would have thought girls would be flocking around you."

He shifted in his seat.

"Sorry," she apologised gently. "Sore point?"

He smiled. "Not really a sore point," he admitted. "Just a bit sensitive for me sometimes."

"Do you want to talk about it?" she asked. "I'm your friend now, not your doctor. Friends tell each other things. Feel free to tell me to mind my own business if you like."

He nodded slowly and smiled at her again. "I fell in love once, only once in my life so far. It was brief and fleeting, but it was real. Almost as soon as it happened, she disappeared from my life never to be seen again. At the time, I thought she felt the same; I'm sure she felt the same, but I lost her. It's as simple as that."

Jacinta reached for his hand across the table and held it gently. "Come on," she coaxed. "Let's pay the bill and walk for a while."

"This is my treat," Cory said, "and no arguments."

They wandered along the waterfront, Cory's favourite route. She held his hand and he enjoyed that. "You have to believe me when I say I'm over it now. It's taken a long time, but I don't feel the heartache when I reminisce."

"And you haven't had other relationships?"

"A couple, but nothing serious," he said. "I never felt the need to tie myself down, and my work was my passion. I love being in the hospitality industry. It's a demanding profession and doesn't leave much time for socialising. For a time, I used it as my excuse not to get romantically involved with anybody. Anyway, what about you? Why haven't you married?"

She smiled. "Never found anybody who could fit the bill. In my student days, medical students were very committed to their studies. It was the engineering students who gained the reputation of womanising and they often visited the student guild on the lookout for unsuspecting females." She laughed. "Most of the boys were just out for sex. That's what young men's hormones do to them. Girls are more discerning."

"Is that so?" he asked light-heartedly.

"Very much so," she said. "I fell for a medic in my final year, but it didn't last. Since then, I just have friends, male and female. You'll have to meet them."

"I'd like that," he told her.

He walked her back to her apartment. "I've enjoyed tonight," he said. "Thank you."

"Me too," she said, "and, Cory?

"Yes?"

"Can we do it again?"

"I hope so. We haven't decided where we are going to travel yet. We have a lot of talking to do."

"We certainly have," she whispered.

He grasped her arms gently and bent to kiss her on the cheek. "Goodnight, Jacinta."

"Goodnight, Cory. See you tomorrow?"

"Come to my place for dinner," he invited. "I'll show you what I have learned over the past fifteen years."

"That would be lovely and I'll bring the wine."

"Six-thirty or seven?" he suggested.

"Perfect. Goodnight," and she was gone.

~ * ~

She arrived on the dot of six-thirty. "Welcome to my humble abode," he greeted her. "Come in and make yourself at home. Aperitif?"

"Can I pretend to be very English and ask for dry sherry?" she asked.

"Of course and I think I'll join you. It's been a while since I had sherry," he said. "Do you mind if I carry on preparing while we chat? These open plan apartments are perfect for entertaining."

"Carry on," she told him. "I might come and watch a genius at work!"

"Oh please don't," he stated amicably. "That's simply too much pressure."

"I know it's going to be perfect. What are we having?" she asked, genuinely interested in Cory's culinary skills.

"I'd like to surprise you with each course," he said. "That way you will eagerly anticipate what is to come, I hope."

Jacinta poured the wine as she waited for Cory to serve the entrée. When he placed a delicate looking mushroom and goat cheese tart in front of her, she gasped. "Wow," she exclaimed. "You really *can* cook."

"I like to think so," he said modestly. "My training would be wasted if I couldn't present a meal fit for a king—well, in your case, a queen."

"It looks delicious."

The main course of roast lamb stuffed with sausage and spinach, potatoes roasted with rosemary and assorted steamed vegetables was followed by a typically Greek decadent dessert—baklava.

"Well done, Cory!" Jacinta enthused. "Had I known you were such a brilliant chef, I would have suggested dinner when we first met."

"Wouldn't that have been unethical?" he asked with a grin.

"Well, yes, but I could always have transferred you to one of my colleagues," she said smiling. "I'm going to have to do that anyway now. I can't have you on my patients' list now we have become friends."

He walked round the table and took her hand. Gently pulling her up from her chair, he held her closely. "Are we just friends, Jacinta?"

She looked into his eyes. "I guess not," she whispered. She closed her eyes and draped her arms around his neck. Lips met, tongues probed, bodies touched and as two hearts were beating as one, she willingly allowed him to lead her to his bed.

Afterwards, they lay quietly in each other's arms feeling the love between them. Cory was the first to speak. "I love you," he said.

"I love you too."

"I told you yesterday that I had been in love only once in my life," he said quietly. "That was true, until now. I want you to know the love I feel for you is every bit as real as the love I felt then, but it's a different kind of love. It is mature love wrought out of friendship and felt deeply within my heart."

Jacinta turned on her side to face him. "You don't have to explain, *agápi mou*. We are both mature people feeling mature love, my darling."

"I will never forget Adele. She awakened my soul to real love. She affected me so deeply that I never felt love again until now. You have re-awakened my soul, sweet doctor..." He traced her face with a delicate finger. "...friend..." He kissed the tip of nose. "...lover." He smiled and kissed her again then suddenly changed attitude. Smiling he said firmly, "Now, to the business of our future."

They sat in bed propped up by pillows and sipping the remainder of their dinner wine as they chatted. "Where would you like to go when we leave Greece?" he asked. "Do you have family to consider?"

"Well," she pondered for a few seconds. "I think America is still the land where the streets are paved with gold, but there is always England—London is apparently wonderful. No family. I was brought up in an orphanage, then a foster home until I went to university. I think my parents must have been students, seeing that I have been blessed with a good brain. It happens sometimes that students have unwanted pregnancies and have to have their child adopted or fostered. I have no hang-ups about being abandoned. I had wonderful foster parents and I am proud of all I have achieved."

"And so you should be, but that's such a sad story. We have both suffered losses in our lives. No wonder we have bonded!" He smiled at the thought and gave her an affectionate hug. "What about Australia?" Cory added. "It's a new country, full of opportunity and we have the skills to take with us."

"I'm open to offers," she said.

"I know that," he said cheekily as he rolled over and cupped her breasts in his hands.

"Hey, cheeky," she chastised. "We are being serious here. I'll have to serve three months' notice. In the meantime, I'll leave the organising to you. Find out what you can about the United States, England and Australia."

"That will be my sole mission," he told her in a workmanlike manner. "And I also need to find out what happened to my mother and my sister."

Nineteen

"Hotel Mediterranean, *boró na sas voithíso*? Can I help you?"

"Good morning," Jake said. "Can we speak in English, please?"

"Certainly, sir. How can I help you?"

"My name is Jake Saunders. My fiancée and I are trying to locate a gentleman by the name of Cory Demetriou whom we believe managed a hotel in Protaras around the year nineteen seventy and probably after that date."

There was momentary silence at the other end of the line.

"Hello?" Jake said. He heard the person catch her breath. "Hello?" he said again.

"Just one moment, please, sir..."

Jake looked at Rodi and shrugged. Covering the mouthpiece he said, "There's something happening here. Don't get your hopes up, but I detected some recognition in her voice when I mentioned Cory Demetriou."

"Hello sir. My name is Irena Drakos. Can you please repeat what you said a moment ago?"

Jake complied with her request as Rodi put her ear as close to the phone as she might in order to hear what was being said.

"May I ask your reason for wanting to contact him?"

"It's personal and I'm not sure who you are, Ms Drakos. I don't mean to be rude, but please understand there are feelings to protect, the feelings of my fiancée and those of Mr Demetriou," Jake explained. "I really cannot tell you the nature of the situation before we speak to Mr Demetriou himself. It would be grossly unfair to him."

"I see, but by the same token, I am not in a position to supply information to you, Mr Saunders."

"I understand, but if you might please tell us if Mr Demetriou is still in Cyprus, or if not, where he is living now. If it eases your concern, my fiancée and I live in Corfu and have come to live here with a view to tracing Cory Demetriou. Hopefully, you might see the seriousness of our quest."

"Oh I see. Well, I think it might do no harm to tell you he was manager here from nineteen seventy until nineteen seventy-five. He left and returned to Athens. I have no further information. He did not give me a forwarding address."

"Forgive me, but he didn't leave a forwarding address, or you're not at liberty to give it to me?"

"Truthfully Mr Saunders, I do not know where he is now. I'm sorry."

"Thank you for your help anyway. We are most grateful. At least we now know that Mr Demetriou is no longer in Cyprus. Our search so far has led us from Corfu to Mount Athos and Athens. If he went back to Athens, perhaps that is where we must go next. Thank you again. Goodbye."

Rodi sighed. "Another setback," she declared. "We've already checked our leads in Athens. What do we do next?"

Jake looked at her with loving eyes. "We get on with our lives for now, babe."

Rodi was horrified. "Are you giving up?" she asked in dismay.

"Of course not, but until we can devote all our time to finding him, we have to work and, with luck, keep nibbling away at any opportunity that comes our way. Who knows? Somebody might just turn up here who has seen him, or at least heard where is has gone."

Rodi sighed again. "In your dreams, Jake," she said. "In your dreams."

~ * ~

By Easter nineteen eighty-two, Rodi and Jake resigned themselves to the fact that they could not move on with the search until the end of yet another holiday season. They did not dwell on it. Work was too demanding to allow their minds to wander. Visitors came and went and by the beginning of October, they were both exhausted.

"I don't think I feel like packing up and jetting off to Athens again," Rodi announced at the end of the season party.

"That's fine by me if you are happy with it," Jake said. "Don't be moaning about it, though, come Christmas."

She nudged him playfully. "Would I ever?" she said laughing.

"Yes, you would," he replied, equally playfully.

"Why would you want to be going away again, you two?" Paula asked. Paula was an English member of the team who had joined just before Rodi and Jake had gone to Halkidiki. "You were away for weeks last time and then you went home to England. You have such a beautiful home here. Why would you want to leave it every year?"

Rodi liked Paula. She was like her best friend in Corfu, but she had never disclosed details of the search for her father to her. "Jake's family are still in England, Paula. We have duties," she explained.

"But they could come here just as easily as you go there," Paula suggested. There was no antagonism in her tone.

Jake went to sit by Paula and quietly advised, "Don't go on about it, Paula. It's just something we need to do, but not this year. We are staying home during the closed season and we'll enjoy that. How about you? Don't you want to go home for Christmas?"

"No," she replied quietly. "Nothing for me to go home for. I have Roberto here now." She smiled shyly. "He asked me to move in with him."

"Get away with you!" Jake exclaimed. "Italian Roberto? Our singing waiter? Fantastic! When did all this happen?"

"Early in the season. We just clicked. I think I'm in love," she said longingly. "He makes my heart beat faster than..."

"Whoa there, girl. Too much information," Jake said, laughing. "Anyway, where is he?" he added looking around the room for the handsome Italian.

"He had an errand to do, he said, and he'll be here later," Paula explained.

Jake looked towards the door. "Here he is now," he announced as Roberto arrived with an enormous bouquet of roses.

He presented them to Paula, who blushed profusely, clearly overwhelmed with the attention she was receiving. Suddenly, he was down on one knee producing a tiny box from his pocket. Cheers and applause echoed round the room, but Roberto held his finger to his lips indicating they needed to be quiet. The company was hushed.

"Paula, the love ofa my life," he said with his charming Italian accent. "Willa you marry me?"

Cheers erupted again and Paula's answer was drowned out, but the way she was in his arms and kissing him passionately, told them she had accepted.

"Well, well," Jake said to Rodi as they walked home from the hotel, "that was very unexpected, but how lovely for them."

"I thought it was very sweet," Rodi agreed, "but then I think Italians have the edge on being the most romantic men in Europe."

"I thought Frenchmen held that distinction," Jake replied. "But having said that, I'm sure Englishmen can be romantic too."

Rodi laughed. "Are you fishing for compliments?" she asked.

"Might be," he said coyly.

"Darling, you are my dream guy, the most romantic guy I have ever met. I love you and romance comes easy when you are in love."

Jake smiled. "It sure does, baby."

When they arrived at their white house overlooking the bay, the moon was shining on the sea and displaying the most romantic vista they had ever seen. Jake gasped. "Made to order for my darling Rodi," he said. "I know you said you wouldn't marry me until we found your father, but will you reconsider, baby? Will you marry me in spring here in Corfu?"

Rodi looked at him with love. "Ideally I would want my father to give me away, but I'm not sure he would want to. Realistically how could I be sure he would accept me as his daughter? I might be living in dreamland in thinking he'll be happy to recognise me as such. Darling Jake, I will marry you in spring and we'll have all your family here to witness it. We love each other and that's all that matters. Seeing Paula and Roberto tonight made me realise we should make our wedding plans now. A spring wedding it is, darling."

Twenty

Athens 1977

Cory went to the department of public records in Athens and asked if there was any information about his mother and sister having left the country. He produced all necessary documentation—birth certificate, passport and his father's death certificate.

"Their names are Eleni and Ariadnê Demetriou. I think they would have left round about nineteen fifty-nine or sixty," he explained. "That's when my father passed away and it all happened at the same time," he told the officer.

"How sad," she commented.

"It was," Cory agreed. "I haven't seen my family since then. I would dearly love to know where they are."

The young woman searched the records beginning, on Cory's instructions, at October nineteen fifty-nine. "There is nothing here listed for that time," she told him as she heaved a second volume onto the desk. "These are the departures for January and February nineteen sixty."

Cory strained to see the list.

"There is nobody with the name Demetriou who left at the time you suggest. I'm sorry."

"Might they have gone by air? Are there records of airline passengers?" he asked.

"These records are of those persons who left the country regardless of their mode of transport," she advised him. "Where would the port of departure have been?"

"Corfu," he said. "Definitely Corfu."

"Then I suggest you contact the office of public information in Corfu. They would perhaps have come to Athens in transit, but if they actually emigrated from Corfu, the records will be there. Good luck."

When he returned to Jacinta's house where he had been living for the past three months, he pondered on the situation while he waited for her to come home from work. *Jacinta will know what I should do. She always looks at things clinically. I can't be objective about these personal issues. The thought of going back to Corfu after seventeen years does not inspire me with confidence at all.*

"Do you have to go back there?" Jacinta asked. "We could always telephone."

"I know that," Cory said, tension showing in his eyes, "but are they going to give out such information over the telephone?"

"Cory, calm down," she told him firmly. "You always react before thinking things through. Telephoning is certainly worth a try."

"I know," he agreed. "My mother was the same. We never look before we leap! It must run in the family. If we ever have children, let's hope they take after you! It's a clear case of not engaging brain before mouth is in gear."

She laughed and nudged him playfully. "Let's find a place to live first. I can't hand in my notice until we know where we are going. In the meantime, get onto the telephone directories and find the number for the Corfu office of public information."

"I wanted to talk to you about Australia," he said. "It seems they are keen to welcome immigrants with good qualifications—some jobs more than others. You'll be fine. Doctors are always needed. You'll just have to get your qualifications assessed, but I'm certain there won't be a problem."

"What about you?"

Cory's eyes sparkled with excitement. "I'm going to open a delicatessen. I have the capital from my savings and from the money my father left me. I never touched it because I knew eventually I would want to do something like this. Apparently there is a big Greek community in Melbourne. Maybe we can apply to go there? What do you think?"

"I think we should," she told him excitedly. "Let's start the ball rolling tomorrow. I have the day off so we'll go to the Australian Embassy and see what we have to do."

~ * ~

"Department of Public Information. How can I help you?"

"Good morning. My name is Cory Demetriou..."

"Cory Demetriou? My god, Cory, how are you? It's Tia Nikolaus, now Giannopoulos. Do you remember me?"

"Tia?" Cory felt his face burning. "Of course I remember you. What are you doing in Corfu and more to the point, what are you doing in the office of public information?"

"My husband's job brought us out here in nineteen seventy-one. It was only supposed to be for two years, but we liked it so much, we settled in Kokkini. When I left the hospitality course, I transferred to social studies. So many doors opened for me then."

"Such a long time ago, but I can hardly believe it. I know Kokkini well. Good for you, Tia. What does your husband do?"

"He's an engineer. He works for the Corfu Water Authority. We now have two children, too. Anatole and Stephanos. They are wonderful little boys."

"Congratulations. It would be great to catch up, but I'm calling to see if you have any information about my mother and my sister, Eleni and Ariadnê Demetriou. They disappeared about October nineteen fifty-nine. Is it possible that you might know if they left Corfu and if so, where did they go?"

He heard Tia sigh.

"We wouldn't normally give out such information over the phone, Cory, but since I know you, I'll see what I can find out. Leave it with me. Let me have your number and I'll call from home. That way I won't get in trouble for bending the rules a bit."

"Please don't put yourself in an awkward position because of me." His thoughts harked back to what he had done to her and yet it was obvious to him she was not bearing any grudges.

"Don't worry. It'll be fine. I'll call later. Just give me a couple of days."

"Thank you, Tia. Thank you very much. Speak soon. 'Bye."

"No problem. 'Bye, Cory and good to talk to you."

Two days later Tia phoned with the news. "It wasn't easy because your mother left using her maiden name, but it seems they migrated to Australia."

"My goodness! Australia? Thank you, Tia," he said appreciatively. "Do we know which city?"

"It appears they were bound for Melbourne. Good luck, Cory. I hope you find them. Have a good life."

Jacinta came home to the good news. "We are going to Melbourne," he announced. "We'll go back to the Australian Embassy and submit our official application. Give in your notice, Doctor Rodino. Australia, here we come!"

In January nineteen seventy-eight, Mr and Mrs Cory Demetriou left Athens bound for Melbourne, Australia, their whole lives packed up in four suitcases and one shipping container.

Twenty-one

Corfu 1983

The spring wedding of Aphrodite Helena Bartlett and Jake Brendan Saunders took place in the grounds of Hotel Helenya and was conducted by an English celebrant who was a close friend of Jake's family. Greek officials attended to ensure Greek laws of marriage were adhered to and all went well. Rodi looked beautiful in an ivory silk gown designed by one of the students at the Athens School of Arts where Rodi and Jake had been in search of Cory Demetriou. The competition to design her dress was a welcome project for those aiming to break into the fashion industry.

...I'm a qualified teacher, Rodi had written in her letter to the principal of the college. *I understand that design projects would be welcomed by your tutors. I am able to offer two weeks' holiday in Corfu for the winner.*

As a result, she wore the perfect gown and Jake, who had been completely in the dark about the dress, gasped when she appeared at the end of the red carpet on the arm Jean-Paul Bresson, the husband of her mother's friend, Eva. With Jennifer and Mark Bresson as bridesmaid and ring-bearer, as well as her own friend, Lisa and her husband, Damien, Rodi felt she had her family with her on her special day.

The spring weather in Corfu was perfect...warm sunshine with a gentle breeze. With the holiday season not yet in full swing, the hotel ballroom was made available to them for the reception and as a wedding gift, Chef had made the most unusual cake; three tiers of delicious Greek desserts—lemon flavour gelato cake on the bottom tier, tiramisu marbled sponge as the second tier, topped with an incredible profiterole fan filled with fresh cream and strawberries.

"I couldn't have asked for a better wedding day," she said to her new husband as they lay in each other's arms after their first passionate love-making as man and wife.

"It was perfect," Jake told her. "Just perfect."

Rodi smiled. "Not quite prefect..."

"Oh baby," Jake cried. "I'm sorry. That was insensitive of me. Mostly perfect—will that do?"

"Please don't be sorry," she said quietly. "I already said I couldn't ask for a better wedding day and that's true. It was as near perfect as it could be, but I so wanted my father to walk me down the aisle."

"I know, darling and when we find him, we'll renew our vows," he paused and winked at his bride. "Even if we are all walking with Zimmer frames!"

"Thanks, babe," Rodi said smiling. "Jean-Paul was the perfect stand-in and the day was still magical. Thank you."

"For what?" Jake asked curiously.

"For being you," she told him. "Just for being you."

"With words like that, I might just have to show you how much I appreciate you being with me."

"Yes, please," she said invitingly and the honeymoon continued, their desire for each other having no bounds.

~ * ~

With a prolonged honeymoon on hold until the end of the holiday season, Rodi and Jake worked happily and delighted in being able to go home together to the white house in its idyllic setting at the end of each day.

"I know I'm beginning to sound like a broken record, but I don't want to go to Athens at the end of the season," she said one evening when they were relaxing on their terrace with a glass of wine and listening to the chirruping of the cicadas reminding them they were living in a tropical paradise. "We have to see if there is another way of tracing where he went in Athens."

Jake sighed. "Baby, are you tiring of the search?"

Rodi looked at him wide-eyed. "No, I'm not," she cried. "I'm tired of jetting here, there and everywhere and then hitting a brick wall. I wish we could just find a bit of concrete evidence. If I knew Cory Demetriou would be there when we got there, it would be a whole different story."

"But just think how far we've got in the past couple of years."

"Not very far," she grumbled. "I came to Corfu, we went to Lakones, to Mount Athos, to Athens and almost to Cyprus and now we are supposed to go back to Athens. It's so frustrating and..." She paused significantly. "And how do I know he's going to accept me as his daughter anyway? He might even have another family he dotes upon."

Jake took her hand and held it gently. "Baby, you are sounding very negative at the moment," he said quietly. "Let's see how we feel at the end of the season and work it out then."

"Why are you always right?" she asked with sincere affection in her voice. "I do love you, Jake Saunders, and I love the way you always say *'we'* when the problem is really mine."

"We are a team, Mrs Saunders. We share everything, even our problems," he reminded her. "And anyway, 'a problem aired is a problem shared and a problem shared is a problem halved'."

Rodi smiled lovingly at him. "Mum always said, *'No problems; only solutions,'* so I guess I should take a leaf out of her book."

"I think you were at the end of the queue when they handed out patience," Jake suggested.

Rodi laughed. "With lack of patience and putting mouth in gear before brain is engaged, I think I should rub myself out and draw myself all over again!"

"I love you as you are," Jake reiterated. "Warts an' all."

Twenty-two

Melbourne, Australia 1978/79

Cory and Jacinta Demetriou arrived in Melbourne the day after Australia Day in nineteen seventy-eight. They booked a week's stay in a hotel and spent every waking moment looking for jobs and inspecting properties where they might put down roots.

"We must try to find jobs first," Cory said. "That way we'll know where to buy a house."

"I'll go to all the hospitals I can find," Jacinta told him. "I'll probably have to apply through the State Health Authority, but if I speak to hospital administration, I should be able to find out the correct procedure."

"We both speak English. That should help us," Cory said enthusiastically. "I'll try to find a position in a hotel. I won't start looking for premises for my shop until I feel comfortable living and working here."

Jacinta eyed her husband carefully. "What about finding your family, Cory?"

He shrugged. "That can wait; *they* can wait. I need to focus on finding a job and finding us somewhere to live. It's been almost twenty years since I've seen them. What harm can a few more months do?"

Jacinta knew he was right. "You know, *sweetheart*," she stated affectionately. "When I first met you, you were such an afraid little boy with no confidence about you at all after the Cyprus thing. When I look at you now—happy, confident, totally in command of your life, I see the man with whom I fell hopelessly and completely in love. I am so proud of you, my darling."

Cory smiled. "You saved me, my darling," he said, his eyes shining. "I was always like this. This is the real me. Cyprus took away my spirit for a while, but now I feel able to live again and..." He paused poignantly. "...and love again. It has been a long time since I felt able to do that. Thank you, darling. I owe it all to you."

Jacinta laughed and nudged his arm playfully. "What is this?" she asked with a grin. "The mutual admiration society?"

"Could be," he quipped. "And why not?"

~ * ~

Cory was the first to arrive back at their temporary home in a hotel with the good news of having secured a job. "I managed to gain a position at the Grand Hotel. They were impressed with my qualifications and offered me a place as assistant manager."

"That's wonderful," Jacinta told him. "Now I must impress the Victorian Health Authority in the same way."

"You'll be fine," he assured her.

Cory's prediction came true. Jacinta was offered a position at the children's hospital. "I need to find a professional translator to transcribe my qualifications before they will officially offer me the job, but I'm assured the post is mine as soon as I am able to provide the necessary documentation."

"Where will we find a professional translator?" Cory asked. "Can't we do it ourselves?"

"I don't know about you, but I don't consider my written English good enough to pass muster with the Health Authority. We'll look in the telephone directory and go to the council offices if necessary. Somebody will know where we can find an interpreter."

When all the legal requirements were carried out, both Cory and Jacinta settled in their new jobs and quickly rented an apartment near to the hospital so that when Cory worked late at the hotel, Jacinta would be able to walk home from work. It didn't take long for them to realise that they would have to work hard in order to establish themselves in the new country. They arrived home exhausted, sometimes like ships that pass in the night. The times when they were home together were so precious that they rarely went out and so it was difficult for them to socialise and make new friends, almost impossible to have a life other than work and sleep.

Cory realised what he must do after working long shifts at the Grand for a year. He started to look for premises to open his shop. His days off were spent trailing around the streets in the café culture districts, sampling what was on offer and weighing up the possibilities of opening his dream shop. He found the very place just off Lonsdale Street. There were already cafés and restaurants there and it was the perfect location for his Greek delicatessen.

Opening day was momentous for him. The *House of Aphrodite* embodied everything he wanted to display: "Aphrodite was the goddess of love, beauty and pleasure. She personifies everything I desire in providing my customers with the authentic food of my homeland. When you come into my store, I hope you will sample the delights of Greece before you take home whatever your heart desires. Welcome to the House of Aphrodite." His presentation to the invited guests at his grand opening was greeted with warm applause and loud cheers.

Jacinta stood among the crowd and beamed with pride. Many of them were Greek and it was the first time she had communicated in her mother tongue, apart from with Cory, since she arrived in Australia. "*Syncharitíria, thavmásios,*" they said joyfully over and over again. "Congratulations, wonderful."

The House of Aphrodite had been open for about six months. He had trained his staff to produce the most wonderful Greek fare and the reputation of the Greek delicatessen had spread throughout Melbourne. It was frequented by many of the Greek community and the restaurants and cafés in and around Lonsdale Street patronised the store for the best Greek foods, particularly pastries.

When a lady asked to see the owner personally, Cory's manager explained, "He isn't here this morning, but he will be in this afternoon if you would like to come back about two o'clock," the store manager said. "May I give him a message?"

"Not really," the lady told him politely. "My husband and I would like to discuss business with him. We'll both come back this afternoon. May I make an appointment?"

"I'll write your name in the diary and let him know as soon as he arrives," the young man informed her. "That's the best I can do, I'm afraid. Your name please?"

"Scafidi. Mr and Mrs Cyrus Scafidi."

~ * ~

"I asked them to come back at two o'clock. Is that all right?"

Cory looked at his watch. It was a quarter to two. "Yes, I guess so," he said. "I can always offer them tea and pastries. I haven't had lunch. Tracking down supplies took longer than I anticipated. What did you say their name is?"

"Scafidi."

"Cory smiled. "Good Greek name anyway. Let's hope we can do business with them. At the rate we're going, I'll need to open another store soon."

The Scafidis arrived promptly at two. The manager showed them to a table by the window, but private enough for business to be discussed. "Would you like tea?" he asked as he placed the chair for Mrs Scafidi to sit.

"Thank you. That would be lovely," she replied. "Cyrus?"

Cyrus, a portly gentleman of around sixty-five years old, grunted a little as he sat down, but agreed that tea would be nice. "And I'll sample some of the pastries I've heard so much about. Thank you."

Cory came out of the preparation room and walked towards the table by the window. He smiled at the portly gentleman who sat facing him and noted his wife who had her back to him, appeared to be very well dressed and extremely well-coiffed. Cyrus Scafidi stood as Cory approached at the table. "Are you the owner?" he asked without ceremony.

"I am," Cory said equally without ceremony.

"I'm Cyrus Scafidi and this is my wife..."

What happened next couldn't possibly have been anticipated. Cory was absolutely stunned, but found sufficient aplomb to gasp flatly, "Eleni..."

Mrs Scafidi turned at the sound of her name. "Cory? Oh my god, Cory. Is it really you?"

"Do you two know each other?" Scafidi asked completely confused.

Cory took a deep breath. "You could say that," he said, anger rising from deep within his soul.

Mrs Scafidi picked up a napkin from the table and fanned her face that was rapidly becoming extremely flushed. "I think we have some talking to do," she offered, her voice weak and trembling.

"We do indeed, Mother," Cory spat.

"Mother? What do you mean...mother?" Scafidi asked, his own face becoming flushed as he tried to work out what was going on with these two people whom he thought had never met.

"I think you had better come into my office. Our conversation will be private there," Cory suggested. "Rob, this may take a while. I won't be available for the rest of the afternoon. I'll leave everything in your hands. You know the ropes."

The manager, Rob, nodded with a look of surprise on his face. "No problem, Cory."

The three people who had just met took their leave and went to the office where Cory signalled for his visitors to take a seat in front of his desk.

"What is going on?" Scafidi asked. "I think I need an explanation, Eleni."

"It seems my mother isn't good at explanations," Cory stated harshly.

Eleni sniffed and trembled. "I don't know where to begin."

"At the beginning," both men said at the same time.

Eleni's voice was low. "I guess it starts with Ariadnê. I became pregnant before Petros and I were married. I don't think I would ever have married him had I not been having his baby. Our parents forced us to marry and it wasn't bad at first. The thrill of having a husband and a baby was every girl's dream. Petros worked hard, I'll give him that, but he was never a good husband. As long as I did what he wanted, he was happy and I just went along with it because I thought that's what I was supposed to do."

"But you told me you never married," Scafidi said, not hiding his contempt.

"I know," she continued, "and I'm not proud of what I told you. Having a child out of wedlock isn't something I wanted to make public, but when I arrived in Australia, I thought that was the best story to tell. We considered that Australians were much more open-minded than Greeks in a tiny Corfiot village. Ariadnê agreed and we always stuck to it. I didn't want Petros to find me. He always resented having a daughter when he wanted a son."

"I don't like where this is going, but go on," Cory urged. "It's better I know the whole truth even though I anticipate it will be hurtful."

"You lied to me, Eleni," Scafidi grunted. "How could you do that to me?"

"Please, sir," Cory pleaded. "You and my mother can sort out your problems in the privacy of your own home. Here in my shop, I need my mother to explain to me why she left Corfu and why she didn't contact me in twenty years to let me know that I still had a mother and a sister."

"Would you prefer me to leave you two alone?" Scafidi asked, visibly shaken at what was unfolding.

"No, don't leave, Cyrus," Eleni cried. "I need you to listen."

Scafidi settled back in his chair, noisily puffing and panting as if he had just run a marathon.

"Cory, you were so close to your father as you were growing up that you didn't notice how he treated Ariadnê and me," she continued. "I'm not blaming you, but your father had no respect for me and I considered at the time he had no respect for women in general. He gave me just enough money to live on; nothing more, nothing less. When I had you, he was thrilled I'd given him a son and he found no further reason to show me any affection for the rest of the time we were together..."

Cory put his head in his hands. His mind wandered back to his childhood and his teenage years. *I knew there was no love between my parents even when I was only a child. My father worked long hours and was often drunk when he came home. Oh, he never had a wrong word to say to me, but he did criticise Ariadnê a lot and I was too selfish to defend her. My goodness, how maturity makes us see the error of our ways.* He looked sadly at the woman in front of him. He remembered her as a good mother, but in hindsight, she had always seemed to be unhappy.

Why are you only working this out now, Cory? he asked himself silently. *Blocking from your mind the woman who gave you life isn't admirable, but that's what you have done for the past twenty years.* He shook his head slowly. *I was angry, very angry. I ought to have been more understanding. Jacinta helped me find my spirit again after Cyprus, but how could she know the anger for my mother was still there inside? My heart goes out to my mother now—maybe twenty years too late.*

"...so you see, I disappeared without a word because I had to leave Corfu and all my unhappiness behind. At this moment, it seems very selfish of me, very weak and extremely uncaring to abandon my son. It's such a long time ago and even now I feel the hurt of all the abuse I suffered. Your father never hit me, but he was cruel and vicious in many ways, often too subtle for anybody else to notice.

"The night I left, we had the most awful row before he went to work and that's what gave me the incentive to put my plans into action." She sighed deeply. "I'm sorry, Cory, but if I might say something in my defence, I knew you would survive without me. You had left home anyway and your father would never hurt you the way he hurt Ariadnê and me. Had I told you about the escape I had spent years planning, I didn't trust that you wouldn't tell your father.

"Please believe me when I say it wasn't really you I didn't trust, it was the man whom I had married and who had always treated me like a plaything, something he could discard when he didn't want it anymore—that's how it always felt to me. If I had kept in contact with you, there was always a danger Petros would follow me if he found out and I would have killed myself if that had happened."

Scafidi stirred uncomfortably in his seat. "Eleni, I wish I'd known all this before. We could have sorted it. Now I'm not so sure we can."

"What do you mean?" she asked with fear in her eyes.

"Because you are a bigamist!" he cried desperately. "We will be in a whole lot of trouble when the authorities find out. I loved you twenty years ago, I love you now, but I don't think love will solve this massive problem however strong it might be."

Cory couldn't help but smile.

"What is there to smile about, Cory?" his mother asked, showing some displeasure that her son would make light of her situation.

Cory stood up and walked round to where Eleni was sitting. He knelt at her feet and took her hands in his. He looked into her eyes and saw panic, fear and desperation, but for a brief moment, he saw the love of a mother for her son and he held on to that as he said quietly, "I should have done this years ago. I should have looked into your eyes and told you I love you because you are my mother. My own life has not been easy, but as you predicted, I did survive." He squeezed her hands gently and then said, "You are not a bigamist."

"She's not?" Scafidi cried in sheer relief.

"The night you left, *bampás* was killed in a road accident."

Eleni gasped and tears ran down her face.

"He was very, very drunk and I have to say, he must have been shocked that you had left. He apparently wandered drunkenly round Lakones shouting after you, and not too kindly from all accounts," Cory explained gently.

"I can well imagine," Eleni said clearly. "He never had a good word to say to me or about me, but I never wished him dead. I'm sad his life ended in that way."

"He was killed outright when a car came around the corner and didn't see him," Cory continued. "It was horrendous at the time and I was in a bit of a mess, but Antonis—do you remember him?"

"I do," she interrupted briefly. "Didn't he go to Mount Athos to take up the monastic life?"

"Yes, he did," Cory went on. "I went on retreat to help manage my grief, not just of losing Dad, but also you and Ariadnê. Antonis was so kind to me and when I left Mount Athos I knew I would survive, I just knew."

"Poor love," his mother said with true motherly sympathy. "I hope we can start again. Ariadnê will be so pleased. She has often had a private word in my ear about you. We never forgot you, Cory. You have to believe that."

"We have a lot to catch up and I'll organise dinner at our place as soon as possible," Cory said smiling. "You have no idea what a difference this will make to my life."

"Our place?" his mother asked. "You are married with children?"

"Married, but no children. Jacinta and I only married just before we came out here."

"Jacinta? A good Greek girl then?" she asked with a smile. "We'll look forward to meeting her."

Scafidi stood up and shook Cory's hand. "I came in here to discuss business and I'm leaving with a son!" he joked amiably.

"Perhaps we can come back next week and explain the plans we envisage for our hotel and your deli supplies. Have you ever catered for Greek weddings? We might as well keep it in the family!"

Twenty-three

During the holiday season of nineteen eighty-four, Rodi and Jake put the search to the back of their minds. Visitors from England seemed to come in quick succession and although family and friends looked after themselves, it was still a strain not to have their own space all summer. Rodi began to feel unwell around the middle of August and Jake advised her to take a few days off.

"But how will you cope?" she asked him. "All my children's reps are new this season. How can I leave them on their own?"

"Rodi relax," Jake said despairingly. "Nobody is indispensable, even when we think the hotel will fall apart without us. Put Lindsay in charge. She has shown a lot of initiative and she only has to make sure the programme goes off without a hitch."

"Are you saying that's all my job entails?" Rodi interrupted, her irritation with Jake's assessment evident in her tone.

"Of course not," he snapped.

"No need to snap, Jake," she retaliated. "It was a perfectly valid observation."

Jake sighed. "What's got into you, Rodi? These last few days you've been like a bear with a sore head. Have I done something to upset you?"

Rodi burst into tears. "No, it's not you, babe," she told him. "I just feel so tired and sickly at the moment. I might have picked up a bug. Bugs thrive in this climate. I *will* take a couple of days off. I'll go and see the doctor in the morning. Hopefully he'll give me something to take away this awful feeling."

She had to drive to Corfu Town to see the doctor. She went early so as to be there and back before the heat of the midday sun affected her. When Jake arrived home that night, Rodi was lying on the terrace in the cool of the evening breeze coming in from the sea. She looked pale, but more relaxed than when he had left for work that morning.

"Are you all right, darling?" he asked as he bent to kiss her. "What did the doctor say?"

"He told me lots of things," she said matter-of-factly.

"Didn't he give you something to make you feel better?" he asked, feeling concerned now that Rodi was really sick and needed looking after.

"There's not much he *can* give me," she said.

"Why not? What sort of a doctor doesn't prescribe medicines?" he questioned crossly.

Rodi pushed herself up and made herself comfortable. "The kind that tells me I'm going to be a mummy!"

Jake was shocked; momentarily struck dumb. "Are you kidding?" he asked warily. "I'm going to be a daddy?"

Rodi nodded and smiled the disarming smile Jake had seen when she first appeared asking for a job. He took her in his arms. "Well done, sweetheart. Congratulations! Didn't you do well?"

Rodi laughed. "Didn't *we* do well?" she corrected. "It takes two to tango, you know."

"That puts paid to our trip to Athens good and proper, doesn't it?" he said with a grin. "Did you know you might be pregnant when you said you didn't want to go?"

"No I didn't. I should have realised I was overdue, but because of the busy summer we've had, I never noticed. Silly I know, but it's the truth."

"Well I'm delighted and it looks like we'll need a new children's rep next season."

"I'll be happy with that, but I'll be well enough in a few days to finish this season." She kissed her husband on the cheek. "Now please, will you make your pregnant wife a cup of tea?"

~ * ~

The baby was born on Rodi's birthday, the twenty-sixth of May nineteen eighty-four.

"Looks like we're setting a family tradition," she joked. "First my father, then me and now our son. It has to be a good omen. Cory Bartlett Saunders has mapped out our future."

Jake hugged his wife with all the love and affection he had for her and the baby. "He has my hair and your eyes, but I don't know whose nose he has," he said as he looked adoringly at his firstborn.

"I think it's his own nose," Rodi said. "It's a beautiful little button nose, a quarter Greek and three quarters English."

"Ah, but that's not right," Jake said firmly. "He's a quarter Greek, a quarter Irish and half English! Blimey, what a mixture!"

"The main thing is he's ours, yours and mine. He was made of our love and he'll have a mummy and a daddy all his life. That means more to me than anything." Rodi wiped a tear from her eye and Jake held her close while she wept with happiness for the little life they had created.

Rodi took to motherhood with ease. The first few months were demanding, but not draining. Jake went to work and came home each night to a loving wife and a smiling, cooing baby. Rodi reported everything she noticed about Cory when Jake arrived home.

"He said ada-da-da today," she said one evening after she had put him to bed.

"Did he?" Jake said. "Brilliant."

"I was a bit brassed off," she told him. "Here I am looking after him day in, day out, feeding him, changing him, talking to him, playing with him, taking him for walks along the headland and round the village and what is his first word?" She placed her hands on her hips and stated with indignation, "Ada-da-da! Not ama-ma-ma, but ada-da-da!"

Jake laughed out loud. "Ha-ha-ha! He's his daddy's little boy! We men must stick together!"

"Well that's all right so long as you both appreciate mummy together too," Rodi said, laughing with him.

"That surely goes without question, babe." He looked lovingly at his beautiful wife. "I love you more and more each day. Always remember that."

~ * ~

Just before Cory's first birthday, Rodi took him to Corfu Town for his check-up. She pushed his pram through the narrow streets near the harbour, she stopped to look in a window that displayed posters of Sydney, Australia. 'New Country, New Life.' *That was my ambition at one time. Australia is very inviting, but no thanks, not now, not until we find my father and the search must begin again soon. My journal has been massively interrupted and it needs a conclusion one way or another,* she said silently and carried on to the doctor's surgery. The waiting room was full of elderly gentlemen, middle aged women, mothers and children, mothers and babies. She took her place in the queue next to a woman with a teenage boy. They nodded to each other and the lady said something in Greek to her.

"I'm sorry, but my Greek isn't very good," she said with a smile. "I am learning, but not very successfully at the moment." She indicated that the baby was taking up all her time.

"What his name?" the lady asked in broken English.

"Cory," Rodi told her.

The lady smiled. "I once knew somebody called Cory. We met at university in nineteen sixty-one. Long time ago. He live in Australia now."

"I always wanted to go to Australia," Rodi confided. "I was looking at a poster of Sydney in the travel agency window just before I came in here. Still, here I am in Corfu and I love it."

The lady looked wistful. She nodded slowly, her eyes sparkling at whatever she was thinking. Quietly she said in a voice barely above a whisper. "Yes," she said with a smile on her lips. "Cory Demetriou."

Rodi couldn't believe what she had just heard. "Did you say Cory Demetriou?" she asked wide eyed. She could hardly contain her emotions.

"Yes," she said louder now. "You know him?"

Rodi's heart leapt in her chest. She could hardly breathe, but managed to say, "My name is Rodi Saunders and I would love to talk to you about Cory Demetriou if you don't mind. May we meet for coffee sometime soon? I will bring my husband, whose Greek is much better than mine. You have no idea how you may have changed my life. Please Mrs...? Sorry I don't know your name."

"Tia," the lady told her. "Tia Giannopoulos."

~ * ~

Rodi didn't wait for Jake to arrive home from work. She went straight to the hotel and found him with Paula supervising a guests' water polo match.

"What are you doing here?" he asked as he took Cory in his arms and hugged him close. "Is the little fella okay?"

"Yes, he's fine. Doctor checked him out and he says he's healthy and doing everything he should be doing at his age," Rodi said. "Can you spare a few minutes. It's important."

"Can you cope, Paula?" he asked his assistant.

She nodded and said, "You go and see what Rodi is obviously excited about." Then to Rodi. "You're not having another baby, are you?"

Jake looked shocked, but Rodi jumped in quickly with, "No, I am not! One is more than enough at the moment."

"Phew," Jake said with relief.

"Come on love," Rodi encouraged. Let's go and you can tell me what this is all about."

"You'll never guess what has happened," she gabbled. "I was sitting in the doctor's waiting room and the lady next to me..."

"Slow down, baby," Jake said, "and get to the point."

Rodi took a deep breath and related the incident to Jake.

"You are joking!" he exclaimed. "No wonder you are excited. What did you tell her?"

"Nothing really," she explained. "I just asked if we could all meet for coffee sometime soon so that we might talk about Cory Demetriou. Tia's English isn't that good and I told her your Greek was better than mine. Oh Jake, I can't believe it. Who'd have thought we would find information out of the blue like that?"

"Does she know where he lives?" Jake asked, almost as excited as Rodi.

"Oh, I didn't give you that bit of important information in my rush to tell you the rest," she said more seriously now. "He's in Australia."

Jake's jaw dropped. "Oh my goodness," he wailed. "We were saying we didn't want to go to Athens, but Australia? Way off our radar, sweetheart. This needs some digesting, doesn't it?"

Rodi looked disappointed with Jake's reaction. "We'll work it out, darling. We have managed so far and this has to be the best lead we have had since we started searching," she told him. "Go back to work now and we'll talk when you come home. I have Tia's phone number so we'll arrange to meet for coffee when you are free."

~ * ~

Rodi left Cory with Paula and Roberto when they went out to coffee on the following Saturday morning. She wasn't sure how much information she would be able to glean from Tia Giannopoulos, but she was very excited all the same.

"Don't get your hopes up too high, Rodi," Jake advised. "I know you and you'll be devastated if we don't find out what you are hoping for."

"Look, darling, we already know he's in Australia. That's a massive leap forward in our search," she stated sensibly. "Any more information, however small, will be a bonus."

They arrived at the *taverna* in the old part of Corfu Town where Tia had suggested. Tia and her husband were already there and stood to greet them. "*Yiasas*," she said. "*Ti kanete?*"

"*Yiasas*," Rodi returned the greeting. "*Eímaste kalá*. We are well and that's just about the extent of my ability to speak Greek! This is my husband, Jake."

Tia smiled. "My husband, Colum. He speak English more good than me," she said. "We leave it to the men, hey?"

"We shall," Rodi agreed warmly, "but we'll help when necessary. Shall we order coffee?"

Colum's English was indeed very good. "I'm an engineer," he explained. "We need English. Some of the best feats of engineering genius were English and I studied in London for a little while."

"Well, that lets me off the hook a bit," Jake said with a sigh of relief. "I am most grateful I don't have to struggle through with my very basic knowledge of Greek. Thank you very much, Colum."

"It is my understanding you wish to know about Cory Demetriou," Colum began. "Would it be too rude to ask why?"

Jake looked at Rodi for reassurance. "I'll take it from here," she said.

Briefly she explained about her mother's will. Tia and Colum listened in silence. "...I never knew the name of my father until my mother passed away. The past four years have been spent searching for him. You can no doubt imagine my shock when Tia mentioned his name."

Tia was the first to speak and Colum interpreted. "Cory told my friend's boyfriend that he had been in love and didn't want to fall in love again. He said the heartache when it all fell through was too much for him. I liked him when we were at college, but he didn't like me in that way." She smiled at her husband. "Then I met Colum and the rest is history."

Colum touched her arm and then continued. "Tia received a phone call at work. It must be about eight years ago now. It was Cory, searching for his mother and sister..."

"We knew they had disappeared. I hope he found them," Rodi said wistfully.

"We think he must have by now," Colum told them. "Tia was able to tell him they had migrated to Melbourne, Australia. The outcome was, Cory and his wife followed them out there. He obviously did fall in love again and got married. That's all we know."

"Oh my goodness!" Rodi cried. "It looks like I missed him only by three years. I arrived in Corfu in nineteen eighty-one. If he left in nineteen seventy-eight..."

"He was in Athens," Tia informed her. "He wasn't in Corfu."

Rodi sighed and shrugged wistfully. "If only Mum had told me about him."

Jake interrupted. "Don't go down that road, Rodi. It won't serve any purpose."

Rodi knew she couldn't turn back the clock. "I just wish..."

"Thank both of you," Jake said finally. "We have so much to take in now and to discuss before we might make the next move. Our task is enormous."

"We are pleased we could help and we hope all your dreams come true, Rodi," Colum said. "Please let us know how you get on."

"We shall and thank you again," Jake said.

"Thank you. I can't tell you how grateful I am," Rodi said. She smiled warmly and wished them well as they left.

Twenty-four

"I don't know how I feel," Rodi declared when they arrived back in Paleocastritsa. "We have so much positive information we have waited so long for, but we now have a big dilemma which I can't consider logically at the moment."

"What do you mean, babe?" Jake asked. "I thought you'd be over the moon to know your father is definitely in Melbourne. All we have to do is track him down."

"And how do you suggest we do that?" she asked, her voice full of despair. "We live in Corfu; we have a young child; you have a job you love, a very demanding job. How can we go to Australia? It's at the other end of the world."

"Let's sleep on it," Jake suggested. "Problems don't seem half so bad when you wake up in the morning. We'll work it out, I promise."

"I know you are right as usual," she conceded, "But I'm not sure I'll get much sleep. My mind is buzzing with what we have learned today. I had almost convinced myself before we met Tia and Colum that we might not be talking about the same person..."

"What?" Jake asked. "Why?"

"There could be more than one Cory Demetriou in the world," she explained. "It wasn't until Tia mentioned about his mother and sister that I was completely sure we were on the same page. Thank goodness for that." She sighed deeply.

After dinner, with Cory fast asleep, she snuggled close to Jake and said, "Let's have a glass of wine. I need to relax."

Jake smiled lovingly. "I know a wonderful way to make you relax," he said with a twinkle in his eye.

Rodi nudged him deliberately. "Stop being lecherous," she joked, "but I must say, I kind of agree. Come on, let's go to bed."

The following morning, Rodi felt dreadful. "I didn't sleep a wink," she said wearily. "I almost wish we were still considering going to Athens. It would be preferable to the impossibility we are facing now."

Jake looked at his wife and saw despair personified. "My sweet, darling Rodi," he said gently. "Nothing is impossible. I lay awake for most of the night too, thinking of what was indeed possible. We simply cannot give up at the final hurdle. What has got into you?"

"I don't want to give up, Jake, but Australia is so far away and we have too much going on here to abandon our life in Corfu. I used to dream of going to Australia to live. British people could go for just ten pounds a few years ago, but not now."

Jake sat beside her on the sofa and took her hands in his. "Money doesn't come into it, babe," he told her. "If I had to, I'd spend my last drachma on helping you find your father. Hear me out while I tell you what I came up with while I was listening to you tossing and turning and tutting and sighing all night."

"Sorry," she said weakly.

"No problem," he assured her, "but I have a proposition for you. The season finishes at the end of October. That gives us five months from now to save up so we can have a holiday when I finish work. I'm suggesting we go to Australia for three months and see what we might find. It will be spring going on summer in the southern hemisphere, the perfect time to leave our winter behind. What do you think?"

Rodi was utterly astonished. "Are you sure?" she asked wide-eyed.

"Absolutely," he said firmly. "We can have November, December and January there. That means Christmas in the sun and come what may, it will be a wonderful holiday for us as a family. We haven't had a holiday since we had Cory."

Rodi hugged her husband warmly. "You are so wonderful," she enthused. "Just wonderful, magnificent, fabulous, the greatest."

"Hold on a bit, darling," he said laughing. "My head is going to swell if you go on like that and I have to get through the door to go to work."

"All so very true, baby," she said as she kissed him affectionately. "My journal is going to take off again with tremendous enthusiasm and I have an enormous amount of planning to do. Thank you so much. You are the best."

~ * ~

Rodi did indeed plan for their trip. They arranged for Jake's parents to spend the winter in the house in Corfu and they were happy to leave the harsher northern English winter weather behind for three months. Instead of staying in a hotel in Melbourne, Rodi discovered it would be to their advantage to rent a furnished apartment and arranged for the real estate agent to secure one for them. The fact that Tia had invested in a home computer was more than helpful. She was able to find everything they needed, book a hire car for them and make sure they would begin the final leg of their search with as few hindrances as possible. On November fifth, nineteen eighty-six, the Saunders family left Corfu for Athens and then they were on the long flight to Melbourne, Australia.

Just as they were about to leave Corfu, Tia and Colum met them at the airport. "We wanted to wish you a safe journey and we hope you find what you are looking for," they said.

Tia pushed an envelope into Rodi's hand. "Open this on the plane," she said quietly. "I've been doing a bit of research for you. I think you'll find it interesting."

Rodi pushed the envelope into her handbag, gave her new friends a hug and said goodbye. Once they had managed to settle Cory in the cot provided for them, they settled themselves into their reclining seats and held hands tightly. "I am so excited," she told Jake. "I can't believe I am actually going to meet my father at long last. I only hope he is willing to meet me."

Jake smiled. "When he sees you, he'll just melt," he said affectionately. "Who wouldn't want you for a daughter?"

Rodi breathed in deeply. "I have to be realistic, darling. It's going to be one hell of a shock for him. I'm trying to be prepared for any eventuality, but it's so hard. He's married and might have children. He may not want me to disrupt his family and I would have to respect that."

"What was in the envelope Tia gave you?" he asked.

"Oh, I forgot about that," she said, and rummaged through her bag amongst travel documents and passports until she found the long brown envelope. "Here it is." She opened it and found a printout from the computer. "It's an advertisement," she told Jake. "*The House of Aphrodite – Demetriou's Delicatessen. Finest Greek fare for private and commercial businesses. The ultimate in catering for parties and weddings. Telephone: (03) 9386 2007.* Oh my goodness, this is it, baby! My contact number." Tears ran down her cheeks. She snuggled up to Jake and wished with all her heart that the long flight to Melbourne was over.

Twenty-five

Melbourne 1979

When the Demetrious' get-together took place, it was a happy occasion. Cory and Jacinta had moved into their new house in South Yarra and discovered it was only minutes away from where his mother and his sister lived. Ariadnê and her husband and teenage children arrived early.

"I wanted to see how my little brother had turned out after all this time," she said as he opened the door to her.

"Come in," Cory invited, giving her a brotherly hug, but feeling strained. "You haven't changed a bit. This is my wife, Jacinta."

"*Kalosórisma. Ti kanete?*" Jacinta welcomed them in Greek.

"Speak English, please," Ariadnê said quite forcefully. "Our children need to keep up with the Australian children, so we always speak English in their presence."

Jacinta raised her eyebrows. "You don't want them to learn their mother tongue?" she asked.

"They know Greek, of course they do, but since they started school, we have always encouraged them to be Australian," Ariadnê explained. "Now they are at uni we want them to belong, to speak without an accent, to fit in."

Cory interrupted. "What's all this?" he asked. "We haven't seen each other for nineteen years or more and you are worried about accents? Come on, Ariadnê, relax!"

His sister looked embarrassed. "Sorry," she mumbled. "I have tried so hard to be Australian for my kids' sake. When I arrived here at first, my English was very bad. Then I met Myles and he helped me. His family has been in Australia for a long time. His accent had almost disappeared. Not like me. Listen to me. I'll never lose it!"

They all laughed.

"Come on, Mum, chill out" the older boy, Max, said affectionately. "We know we are Greek. We like being Greek. We are proud to be Greek."

"Don't overdo it, Max," the younger boy, Leo, told him. He turned to Cory. "Hi, Uncle Cory. I'm Leo. Good to meet you. How ya doin', mate?" he said with all the deliberately exaggerated Australian enunciation he could muster.

Ariadnê chastised her younger son. "Naughty boy, making fun of your mama."

"Come, let us have a drink while we wait for *Màna* and Cyrus," Cory suggested.

"Mama or mum, Cory, not *màna*! Too Greek. You should know by now. You have been here almost two years..." Ariadnê paused significantly. "How come you don't look for us before now?"

Cory didn't answer and the tension was noticeable. Jacinta came to the rescue and poured out cold drinks for them all. They sat on the deck overlooking the Yarra River. The sun shone on the water in front of them and they watched the rowing crews being put through their paces. The atmosphere was friendly again.

"What do you do, Jacinta?" Myles asked as she handed him a beer.

"I work at the children's hospital."

"Oh you're a nurse, are you?" Ariadnê asked.

"No, I'm not. Actually I'm a..."

Ariadnê was quick off the mark again. "A cleaner, oh I see." Her expression was less than complimentary.

Jacinta laughed. "No, I'm not a cleaner, although the cleaners do have a lot of responsibility in a hospital," she said, trying her best to hide her irritation with Ariadnê's condescending manner. "I'm a doctor."

Silence.

Then—"That serves you right, Ari," Myles said to her. "You should engage your brain before you put your mouth into gear!"

Jacinta laughed. "No offence taken," she assured them. "I'm aware of the same trait in Cory. It came out quite often when we first met. He sometimes doesn't think before he speaks."

"But I'm getting better, darl!" he said affectionately.

Ariadnê clapped her hands with glee. "My little brother has just announced to the family he is an Australian! Well done, darl! I see you have indeed picked up the lingo!"

When Eleni and Cyrus arrived, the family was complete. They sat down to lunch in happy mood. Cory decided to cook for them rather than bring in food from his store. The dining room table was set fit for royalty.

"I wanted to show you I am capable of doing this myself. I don't just rely on my staff to do the work. It took me a long time to perfect my skills," he informed them.

"Well, you've impressed me," Cyrus said after the main course as he leaned back in his chair and patted his portly stomach. "No need to discuss your prospects in taking on the catering for us. It's a done deal!"

"You're sure of yourself, Pop," Max said. "How do you know Uncle Cory wants to take on your business?"

"Max! Behave!" Ariadnê scolded. "You are not a business graduate yet. Wait until you are qualified before you interfere with your poppy's business decisions."

Max shrugged. "Just saying..."

Cory poured himself a glass of wine and joined them at the table before serving dessert. He raised his glass and made a toast, "Here's to family. *Stinygiasou.*"

"*Stinygiasou!*" they replied heartily.

Ariadnê was quiet. "You know, Cory," she said pointedly. "You didn't answer my question earlier. Here you are toasting family yet you never tried to find us in twenty years and when you arrived in Australia, you left it for months. Even then it was only coincidence that Mum and Cyrus went to your store."

Cory looked his sister directly in the eye. "Be careful what you say, Ariadnê. You are treading on dangerous ground." His voice was calm and belied what he was feeling inside.

"What do you mean?" she asked, putting on the innocent little girl's voice Cory remembered from when they were growing up.

She's played the innocent all her life. Nothing has changed then. She must have her own way. His thoughts were sad as he recalled how she used to blame him for everything. *No wonder I gravitated to bampás when she manipulated màna all the time.* "Do you really want me to explain?" he asked. "It might spoil what has so far been a beautiful family occasion..."

"Cory," Jacinta urged. "Calm down."

He nodded and smiled at his wife. "I'm all right," he assured her. "I have learned to keep calm. Ariadnê has forgotten how things were."

"What do you mean?" she asked again.

The boys stood and went out onto the terrace to avoid what was fast becoming an argument. "We'll leave you grown-ups to it," Leo said as they left the table. "You can argue it out yourselves."

"There is no argument, boys. Just a family discussion," Ariadnê told them, but they left anyway.

Cory paced the floor while he collected his thoughts. "I am not about to start a row," he told them. "I just wish to tell you how it is. That way we will all know what happened and we can get on with our lives together in harmony." He breathed in deeply. "Just to put you straight, Ariadnê, you and *màna* left without so much as a by your leave."

Ariadnê cringed at his calling their mother, *màna*, the Greek word she had left behind years ago, but she kept quiet.

Cory continued. "That same night, *bampás* was killed. I was left to deal with everything. I was twenty-one years old and ought not to have been put in that position, but you and *màna* left me to do it all. I had no idea where you had gone. I was angry for a long time. I didn't want to find you and who would blame me? I learned to live with it." He paused significantly. "Now having said all that, when did *you* try to contact me? You knew where I was, but I heard nothing. At least *màna* admitted why she didn't contact me and explained the circumstances of her actions. She didn't question me like you. There were circumstances for me too, but I won't go into what happened to me in Cyprus, otherwise you'll think I want your sympathy..."

Jacinta went to stand by him. She took his hand and squeezed it gently. "You don't have to do this, *agápi̱ mou*. I think Ariadnê has got the message."

Cory sighed. "I need to finish—please, Jacinta." He looked directly at his sister. "When Jacinta had given me the confidence to face life with more enthusiasm, I decided to try and trace you. Fortunately, an old friend from my college days had access to records and found that you had come to Melbourne. We were already making our own plans to migrate anyway, but for me, the fact that you and *màna* were here served to confirm we had made the right decision.

"Don't flatter yourself that we came out here just to find the two people who had deserted me. We had ambitions and I put those first before I intended to look for you. It was my considered opinion that after almost twenty years, a few more months wouldn't hurt. Jacinta did not interfere. She said it needed to be my own decision. You already know about the coincidence of Cyrus wanting to go into business with The House of Aphrodite. That just made things easier for me." He sat down at the table and took a long swig of his wine. "Now you know, Ariadnê, and I hope you are happy." There was no animosity in his tone.

After a brief silence, Myles was first to speak. "My wife doesn't think before she speaks, Cory. I apologise."

Cory smiled. "Thanks, Myles. It runs in our family, so I am told." He walked round the table to where Ariadnê was sitting and took her hand. Pulling her to her feet, he gave her a hug. "No hard feelings anymore, sis." He smiled. "Look, I can speaka the lingo after all!"

Ariadnê looked into his eyes. "I'm sorry, Cory, for everything. I'll make it my life's work to make it up to you. When you and Jacinta have children, I shall welcome them with open arms and be the best auntie in the world."

Amid laughter because of the last remark, the extended Demetriou family sat down to finish dessert. "A perfect ending to a perfect day," Eleni said. "My children and my grandchildren together at last."

Twenty-six

Melbourne 1986

Touching down in Melbourne after a twenty four hour flight was such a relief for the Saunders family. Whilst Cory had slept for much of the time, when he was awake, he was fractious and whatever Rodi and Jake did to pacify him, he wasn't interested. They picked up their hire car and drove to St Kilda where they had rented an apartment for the duration of their stay.

"We really ought to try and stay awake," Jake said, "but losing ten hours has certainly taken its toll on me. How about you, sweetheart?"

"I'm shattered," Rodi told him. "I think we should sleep while Cory is asleep and then sort ourselves out later. It's only eight o'clock so we might sleep until lunchtime and then go shopping. We need to eat and I don't feel like dining out today. Maybe we can have take-away tonight." She looked at her husband with tired eyes.

"Come on then," he invited. "Let's put our heads down while our little man is quiet."

Cory woke up at one-thirty so they managed to catch up on some of the sleep they had lost. Feeling a little refreshed, they wandered down to the supermarket in the spring sunshine. It wasn't hot, but pleasant enough for them to sit on the balcony in the evening and watch the world go by. Rodi and Jake discovered literature in the apartment which informed them St Kilda was famous for its food, entertainment and nightlife. Acland Street, only a few minutes' walk from where they were, was a bustling shopping precinct famous for its cafes, continental cake shops, fashion and second-hand shops. Nearby Fitzroy Street was renowned for its restaurants, hotels and bars and the most famous attraction on St Kilda's beach was the St Kilda Pier.

"It looks like we made a good choice in coming here," Rodi said as she read the information about the town. "There is a lot to do and Cory is going to love the beach and seeing the penguins."

"Penguins in Australia?" Jake asked incredulously.

Rodi read out loud from the pamphlet. "*Originally a seaside resort in Melbourne's early years due to its close proximity to the city centre, St Kilda has developed into a trendy and cosmopolitan suburb. At the end of the pier is a breakwater, constructed for the Olympic Games to provide a safe harbour for yachts. Visitors can walk part of the way on top of the breakwater, or descend to a boardwalk at sea level. Penguins have made this rocky breakwater their home. A network for pathways line St Kilda's scenic foreshore, making it ideal for bicycle riding, skating, jogging and walking. At the southern end of St Kilda, the coastal pathway passes beside the St Kilda Marina which was built in nineteen sixty-nine and features waterfront restaurants and a public boardwalk.*

"There is so much to see and do," she reiterated. "It says here St Kilda is a good base for exploring Melbourne and all it has to offer."

"Sounds wonderful, baby," Jake agreed, "but have you forgotten why we are here?"

Rodi threw a look of complete disdain at her husband. "Don't be ridiculous, Jake. Of course I haven't forgotten," she said sharply. "We need to be fully refreshed before we start looking for my father. There is no way I would be able to cope if I felt tired like I do at the moment. We both need to be at our best."

Jake smiled affectionately. "Just when I think you will jump in at the deep end, you come up with pearls of wisdom like that. Well done, sweetheart. I'm proud of you."

~ * ~

After a week recovering from jetlag, Rodi felt she was ready to continue her mission. "I have mixed feelings," she admitted. "I am desperate to meet Cory Demetriou, but I'm terrified he won't want anything to do with me."

"We have to be philosophical about it, baby," Jake told her gently. "Think about the worst case scenario and then whatever happens won't faze you."

"I'm trying not to get too excited so I won't come across as an inarticulate individual who doesn't know what she's talking about," she explained, "but my heart is beating nineteen to the dozen even now just thinking about it. What will I be like when I actually come face to face with him?"

Jake took her in his arms and hugged her tightly. "We're in this together and I'm with you every step of the way. We have to hope he accepts your story. Just be yourself, Rodi. Hopefully he'll see a lot of your mum in you and realise that you are speaking the truth. It's a pity we don't have any photographs from that fateful holiday. Even Eva couldn't supply any. That's a real shame, but we'll manage."

Rodi knew she had to deal with it. She found The House of Aphrodite in the telephone directory. "Look at this," she called to Jake. "There are six branches of his delicatessens. How do I know which number to call?"

"I guess any of them would be all right," Jake suggested. "Cory Demetriou is the owner so he is the big boss man. Surely somebody will tell you how to contact him directly. Isn't there a head office or something?"

Rodi scanned the list of numbers. "It doesn't say so and the number Tia gave me isn't on this list. Maybe it changed, but I'll call the first number on the list. According to the map, it looks as though it's right in the CBD."

"CBD? How come you are suddenly *au fait* with business terminology?" Jake asked, laughing.

"Since I saw it on this map," she said with a wink. "Look— Central Business District."

~ * ~

"Good morning. How may I help you?" the girl on the phone asked pleasantly.

Rodi took a deep breath. "I wish to speak to Cory Demetriou please," she said making a bold effort to keep her nerves in check.

"I'm sorry, but Mr Demetriou isn't at this store today. He is usually here between eight o'clock and midday every Wednesday."

"Oh," Rodi commented, her disappointed clear in her tone.

"I can make an appointment for you if you like," the girl said cheerily. "He is very amenable and likes to meet all his clients personally."

"Oh, I'm not a..." Rodi thought better of telling the girl she wasn't a client. "...I'm not averse to making an appointment, but is there another way I might contact him other than going to the store?"

"I'm afraid not," the girl said firmly, yet not totally unfriendly.

Rodi sighed. "All right, please make an appointment for my husband and me on Wednesday morning," she said. "We'll look forward to meeting him then."

"Your name please?" the girl asked.

"Rodi and Jake Saunders."

"How are you spelling your name please, Mrs Saunders? It is so unusual. You are obviously English, but your name isn't English, is it?" the girl went on politely.

"R-O-D-I and no it isn't English; it's Greek," she explained light-heartedly.

"Oh I see." There was a brief silence. "Will ten o'clock on Wednesday suit?"

"That will be fine. Thank you." Rodi replaced the receiver and flopped onto the sofa.

Jake who had been playing with Cory in the bedroom while Rodi was on the phone came in to see a picture of complete dejection. "No luck?" he asked warily.

"Same old story," she conceded. "One step forward, two steps back. We can't meet him until Wednesday."

"Well, that's okay, isn't it?" Jake asked brightly. "It gives us a bit longer to formulate our thoughts on what we should say. At least we know we are going to meet him face to face at last."

Rodi couldn't hide her disappointment. "I know that, but I had really psyched myself up to meeting him today. Now I have to try and combat the apprehension for almost another week. I don't know how I'll survive."

"Now you're being melodramatic, Rodi Saunders," her husband stated matter-of-factly. He smiled and nudged her playfully. "How do you think Cory Demetriou would regard a drama queen?"

She had to laugh at herself. "He'd probably throw up his arms in horror, laugh idiotically, and roll around the floor hysterically before wildly declaring…" She paused dramatically. "…it runs in the family!"

"Enough!" Jake said as he held on to his sides to stop them aching with laughter. "If he as much as moves his arms in an upward direction when we meet him, I doubt if I'll be able to control myself."

"Sorry," Rodi apologised, "but I feel better now that I've released the tension. Maybe we should roll around the floor laughing just before we leave home on Wednesday morning."

~ * ~

The next week flew by. Rodi, Jake and the baby spent happy hours on the beach, walking around the botanic gardens, taking Cory on the merry-go-rounds in Luna Park and generally taking in all the tourist attractions as would a family on an annual seaside holiday. When Wednesday came, Rodi was once again overcome by the tension she had spent all her time releasing the few days before. She was extremely quiet and Jake allowed her the space and time for her to collect her thoughts.

"Are we ready for this?" she asked tentatively.

Jake looked at his wife and sympathised with how she was feeling. "Will we ever be ready to take this first step, Rodi?" he asked.

"We have to be," she said quietly.

"Right then" Jake replied in a businesslike manner. "Let's get on our way."

Having packed the holdall with everything they needed for the baby and having secured the happy child in his pushchair, they left St Kilda to find The House of Aphrodite. They anticipated that parking in Melbourne would be difficult so they took the tram from St Kilda and enjoyed the iconic ride into the city. With Cory in his pushchair it was easy to walk to The House of Aphrodite from the tram stop.

Rodi rehearsed in her mind what she was going to say. She had avoided discussing her approach with Jake. "I don't want to plan what I'm going to say," she informed him earlier in the week. "Words never come out as you plan."

"Just be yourself, darling," he advised. "Don't jump in all guns blazing, though. Remember this is going to be one hell of a shock for him."

Arriving at the store, they stopped for a moment to take in what they saw. "This is some delicatessen!" Rodi exclaimed in awe. "It's luxurious, not at all like the delis at home in Worthing! It's like walking into an ultra-super supermarket."

Jake approached the automatic doors and pushed Cory through. Rodi followed, her stomach churning and feeling as though she might collapse at any moment, her legs were so unsteady. *Lord help me,* she prayed silently and she desperately tried to appear calm and confident as she approached the reception/information desk. "Mr and Mrs Saunders to see Mr Demetriou," she told the receptionist.

"Just one moment, ma'am. I'll see if he's available."

Rodi looked at Jake and whispered. "It's just like when we were in Athens. We made an appointment to see the hotel manager and then were told to wait to see if he were available. What's the point of making an appointment if..."

"Sh-sh, Rodi," Jake said in hushed tones. "Don't get yourself irritated before we go in."

Rodi smiled nervously. "Sorry," she whispered. "I'm so nervous."

"I know, babe, but take a deep breath and try to relax."

Twenty-seven

Cory Demetriou was on the telephone when the receptionist knocked on his door. "Can't you deal with it, Ryan? I have an appointment to keep here." He looked up as the receptionist opened the door quietly.

"Your visitors are here, Cory," she whispered.

He nodded and continued to speak on the phone. "Do you need to call the police? Just hold on, Ryan, I need to sort out the situation here." He covered the mouthpiece and spoke to the young woman who had just entered the office. "I'm sorry, I'll have to cancel, I'm afraid. There's an emergency at the Prahran branch. Ryan apparently needs me urgently. I'll have a quick word with Mr and Mrs Saunders." He returned to speak to Ryan on the phone. "I'll be there in half an hour. Hold the fort until I get there, please."

He replaced the receiver and went out to reception. Smiling apologetically, he shook the hands of his visitors. "How are you?"

"Fine thank you," Jake said. "We are pleased to meet you." *Understatement of the decade,* he thought.

Rodi kept quiet. Her heart was beating wildly in her chest. Before her stood this olive skinned, dark haired, tall, handsome man who was her father. His hair was exactly the same colour as her own and she completely understood how her mother had fallen madly in love with him twenty-seven years before. She clung to the pushchair to steady herself.

"I am so sorry, but I need to cancel our appointment. There is an emergency at one of my other stores and I am required to sort it out immediately. I apologise for the inconvenience. May I offer to see you another time?" Demetriou explained.

Rodi looked bewildered; Jake took over. "Oh dear," he said. "I'm sorry to hear that. Will we have to wait another week before we are able to see you? We were rather hoping we might sort out our business today."

"No, not a week," Cory replied. "If we can't fit it in during the day, you may come to my house in the evening." He glanced at the sleeping baby in the pram. "Are you able to get a babysitter?"

"No, we are visiting from England. We don't know anybody," Rodi told him, her voice barely above a whisper.

"From England? My goodness, you are a long way from home," Cory exclaimed. "I can't imagine what you would want to talk to me about. Now I am intrigued, but I really must go. Come at the same time tomorrow and I'll alter my schedule to come back here to see you. Is that all right?"

"That will be fine," Jake told him. "We'll look forward to seeing you then."

~ * ~

"I don't believe this," Rodi complained as they walked back to the tram stop. "What do I have to do to talk to my own father?"

Jake, as ever, was more philosophical. "You actually met him, Rodi," he stated firmly. "You actually came face to face with the guy. That is one major achievement after all this time. You have to agree with that. What was your first impression?"

"You mean after being irritated that he was brushing us aside?" she asked moodily.

Jake sighed. "Rodi, you don't half exasperate me at times. The man has a business to run; not a little corner shop, but a big multi-store business. He doesn't know why we are here, nor does he know what we know, so why would he give us priority over an emergency at one of his stores, whatever that might be? The place could be burning down, or a car off the road could have ram-raided it. Drastic I know, but how are we to know what's gone wrong and needs his immediate attention?"

"You're right as usual," Rodi conceded. "Case of brain and mouth not being in sync again." She smiled. "What's one more day in the whole scheme of things?"

"That's my girl," Jake said tenderly. "So come on now, what were your first impressions?"

Rodi took a few moments before she divulged what she had actually thought when she saw her father for the first time. "To be honest, I was initially struck dumb," she admitted. "If I'd had to speak immediately, I would have sounded like a gibbering idiot! My heart was beating nineteen to the dozen and I was, to put it in the vernacular, gobsmacked."

"I thought as much when I saw your face as you shook his hand," Jake told her.

"Then," smiling, she continued, "I saw what Mum must have seen in him. What a handsome guy he is and did you notice the colour of his hair? It is exactly like mine."

Jake smiled. "I'm sure you must have seen much more than looks."

"I know that," Rodi agreed. "But physical attraction is what you see first. Knowing the real person comes later."

"Why did you say we had travelled from England?" Jake asked. "We have lived in Corfu for the past three years."

"Automatic reaction, I guess. I really don't know," she declared honestly. "I was so flustered, I just said it without thinking. It isn't actually a lie. We do come from England originally. Anyway, I feel better now. I hope I'll have the confidence to open up to him tomorrow."

~ * ~

They woke bright and early the following morning and took the tram again as being the easiest way to travel. Rodi was very quiet and pensive. Suddenly she cursed. "Damnation! Why the hell didn't I think of that before? How stupid can I be?"

"What's the matter?" Jake asked.

"I just thought," she explained. "Why didn't we bring photographs of Mum? It's so obvious. I can't believe I left them all in Corfu. How ridiculous is that?"

Jake too was mystified. "I have no idea why we didn't think of that," he said.

"She didn't have any of the fateful holiday, as far as I know," Rodi told him. "I guess she would have destroyed them as sad reminders. Had I thought of it earlier, I might have asked Eva if she had any. Still, too late now."

"Did you bring the will?" Jake asked tentatively.

Rodi took a deep breath and blew it out forcefully. "No."

"You didn't bring the will?" Jake exclaimed. "You left that in Corfu too? You are unbelievable, Rodi!"

"No, I didn't leave it in Corfu, Jake," she said huffily. "I'm not that stupid. I deliberately didn't bring it this morning. I want to see his reaction first. He might just dismiss me out of hand; he might have a quick temper; he might just be so shocked and demand time to think over what I tell him. I'll just wait and see. I think I can be sure just one meeting won't convince him."

Jake squeezed her hand. "You really have thought it out, haven't you?" he said affectionately. "I thought you would and I didn't want to interfere with what you decided to say and do. That's why I haven't asked."

"Thanks, babe," she replied, squeezing his hand in appreciation. "I knew you wouldn't try to influence me unless I asked you directly."

They deliberately strolled to the delicatessen in order to feel relaxed when they arrived there. The receptionist recognised them immediately and asked them to wait while she informed Demetriou they were there. "Please come through. Mr Demetriou is expecting you."

He stood up from behind his desk when they entered. "Good morning," he greeted them. "How are you today?"

"Fine," they replied in unison.

Demetriou smiled. "So very English," he said. "There is something refined about that reply. Australians are all *good*. I like that you are *fine*. Please take a seat and tell me how I might help you." He looked directly at Jake.

"It's my wife who needs to speak to you," he informed him amicably.

"Oh, I see. How can I help you, Mrs Saunders?"

"Rodi, please," she invited.

"All right, Rodi," he said smiling. "Such an unusual name."

Now it was her turn to smile. "Yes," she agreed. "My name is Aphrodite."

A look of surprise appeared on Demetriou's face. "My goodness," he said, laughing in mock nervousness. "I hope you aren't here to lay claim to my delicatessen empire!"

"Not at all," Rodi said laughing with him. "Your empire is safe, but I think you might be in for a shock." Her tone became more earnest; soft, but serious. "Do you recall a girl by the name of Adele Bartlett?"

Twenty-eight

Cory waited for Jacinta to come home from work. He couldn't relax. He paced the floor checking his watch every few minutes. *Please don't be late today,* he urged silently. *I need to discuss this with you. How the hell do I deal with it?* He sat on the sofa; he got up and walked round the room; he sat on a dining chair by the table; he got up and went to look out of the window; he listened intently for the garage door to be remotely activated by his wife returning from the hospital. Nothing was happening. When he did hear the click of the garage door opening, he jumped almost as if he weren't expecting it. When Jacinta walked in, he ran to her and held her tightly.

"Goodness, Cory, what is happening? Such a welcome and I only left you to go to work this morning!" she said light-heartedly, but she felt the tension in his body. He looked directly into her eyes and she saw a hint of the fear she had seen when she first met him. "Sit down, and tell me what is wrong, sweetheart. Why are you afraid?"

Cory sat on the sofa still holding on to Jacinta's hand. "I'm not afraid, *agapiménos*, truly, I'm not afraid, but I have had such a big shock today and...I'm not sure how to deal with it. I need you to listen, Jacinta, to listen without interrupting."

"All right, I'm listening," she told him.

He breathed in deeply. "Where do I start?" he asked, not needing an answer. "A lovely young English couple, Mr and Mrs Saunders, came to see me today. They brought along their baby and I assumed they wanted catering for a party or something like that. The young lady's name is Aphrodite and I made a joke about her wanting to claim my empire."

Jacinta smiled. "Just a co-incidence, I'm sure. She must have Greek background, though. I'm not sure even Greeks would name a baby Aphrodite these days."

Cory signalled to her to be quiet.

"Sorry," she said apologetically.

"She calls herself Rodi—I quite like the sound of that and if what she has told me is true, she does indeed have Greek background." He stirred uncomfortably in his seat. "It is hard for me to admit this to you, *agapiménos*, but it seems I am her father."

"What?" Jacinta gasped. "How can that be? How can she claim such a thing?"

Cory took another very deep breath. "You remember I told you I fell in love only once before I met you? Adele Bartlett was on holiday in Paleocastritsa in nineteen fifty-nine. She stole my heart and we made love on just two occasions before she went back to England. The dates given to me by Rodi are correct. She actually shares my birthday and so does her little boy."

"Coincidence again, Cory. What on earth is she up to?" Jacinta's voice was low, but very stern.

"I'm inclined to agree, but she says she has been searching for me for five years. She even named the baby after me. There must be some truth in what she says. How would she know my name?"

"If she were conceived in nineteen fifty-nine, she must be twenty-six or twenty-seven by now. Why has it taken her so long to find you? How conniving is it for the mother to send her daughter to look for you now when she could have found you herself as soon as she realised she was pregnant? It sounds very fishy to me. If you want my advice, send her packing unless she is able to provide absolute proof she is your daughter. The long-term ramifications of this, Cory, could be mind-blowing." Jacinta was trying to look objectively at a situation that was anything but.

Cory looked sad. "Don't be too harsh, Jacinta. Adele died from cancer in nineteen eighty-one. Apparently she had never disclosed who the father of her child was, not even to Rodi. Her will contained the information and her final request was that Rodi try to find me and get to know me." He paused and chose his words carefully. "She wanted Rodi to discover the man she met and loved, even though it was for a very short time. She tried to relate her mother's exact words from the will to me. Adele never married. I don't know what to think about that."

Jacinta looked sad too. "Cory, I really don't know what is happening here. I don't know how to react, or what to say. How do you feel about it? After all, it's you who has been put in this extremely unenviable position."

"I'm numb," he admitted. "The young lady is lovely, not demanding. She just wants to meet her father, to carry out her mother's dying wish. What I don't understand is that Adele returned my letters unopened when I wrote to her. She obviously didn't want to continue our relationship. The brief time we had together was everything young love should be and I know we both thought it would last forever. I feel completely confused. There is no other way to describe it."

"We need to sleep on it," Jacinta advised him. "Maybe tomorrow we'll see it in a different light. I love you, Cory, and I don't want this to come between us. If it turns out that Rodi Saunders is your daughter, I am very afraid she will disrupt our life together. Perhaps this is the wrong time to say this, but it isn't likely you and I will have children. My body clock is ticking away and Nature knows when it's too late for bringing a child into the world. I can accept that because all I need is your love.

"Your child, if she is your child, makes me feel threatened. God knows my own childhood was fraught with rags, not blessed with riches so I do understand how Mrs Saunders must have felt growing up without a father. This has to be your call, but personally, I would need hard evidence to accept what she is saying is true."

Cory took her in his arms. "I love you, Jacinta. Nothing will ever take that away. You have to understand that. I asked Rodi for time to digest what she had told me. She promised to let me see her mother's will, which contains a detailed account of Adele's wishes and apparently Rodi, herself, has kept a journal of her search for the past five years. Her own words were, *'I don't want to overwhelm you with all the details today. I know it must be a terrible shock, but I searched for you simply to carry out my mother's dying wish. I won't make unreasonable demands of you. I just want to know that you are my father and you accept me for whom I am.'* Believe me, Jacinta, she is a lovely person and I can't deny her the right of having a father if her claims are true. But how will she ever prove it?"

~ * ~

After a restless night, Cory and Jacinta went to work bleary-eyed, but determined to get on with their jobs without distraction. Safe in the knowledge they were on the same page as far as their love for each other was concerned, they endeavoured to keep their minds on the job in hand, paradoxically happy to be able to go home and tackle their undeniably difficult situation in the evenings.

"Should we call a family conference?" Jacinta asked as they ate dinner several days and numerous discussions later.

Cory shrugged, a look of uncertainty in his eyes. "I have thought about it, but do you really think they will come up with anything constructive? I can just imagine *Màna* being over-enthusiastic about a granddaughter, not to mention a great-grandson and she would be ready to believe anything just because of that. On the other hand, Ariadnê will question everything down to proving the time of conception. She won't be helpful at all, because in spite of her outward show of selfishness sometimes, she is very family oriented and will desperately guard our heritage. I know she wouldn't be happy about welcoming a stranger into the bosom of the family in spite of her declaration earlier of smothering our children with love and affection."

"I still think they should know what is happening," Jacinta told him. "If Rodi Saunders is your daughter, she is part of their family whether Ariadnê accepts her or not. She is your child..." She paused and looked almost scared. "...your legal responsibility..." She stopped abruptly.

Cory jumped in and finished what he thought Jacinta was going to say next. "She has a right to my estate. Is that what you were going to say?"

Jacinta nodded. "She wouldn't be the first person on this earth to appear out of the blue and lay claim to what she considers is rightly hers."

"I can't believe that of her," Cory stated firmly. "If you met her, Jacinta, you would understand what I am saying."

"Cory, Cory, Cory," she exclaimed. "You are being naïve! How do you know the whole thing isn't just an act to gain your affection?" She paused significantly. "And then when she has her foot in the door, she will claim her inheritance."

Cory was trying desperately not to be annoyed that his wife wasn't supporting his view. "I'm telling you, Jacinta, Rodi Saunders is a lovely young woman. She has a beautiful soul. I feel it, just like I felt it with her mother."

Jacinta was surprised at his reaction. "You have already accepted her then? In that case, there is no need to continue this discussion." She stood up from the sofa and began to walk away, but Cory grabbed her hand and pulled her back.

"Don't do this, darling," he whispered gently. "I need your support. I haven't accepted her as my daughter. How can I until I have seen the details of her mother's will and read her journal? There will surely be things in there that will prove or disprove her story. I have to ask her to allow me to read both documents, to give me time."

"Please call a family conference, Cory," she pleaded. "We are both too consumed with the whole affair at the moment. Fresh views might just clarify it for us."

~ * ~

The family were called together the following Sunday. Cory related what he knew.

"Do you believe the girl?" his mother asked gently.

Cory sighed. "In my heart I do, because of the chemistry I felt when she mentioned her mother's name, but my head is telling me to ignore that feeling. Jacinta thinks I'm being naïve, but I have to give Rodi a chance to prove what she is saying is true. If I am her father, I shall have to make up for all the time I wasn't there for her when she was growing up."

"Are you mad?" Ariadnê cried. "Her mother should have let you know she was pregnant at the time. How do you know the baby's yours? She might have had lots of boys. You only just met her when she was on holiday. If she was free and easy with you, how do you know she wasn't like that with other guys? How many other girls did *you* sleep with, Cory? There could be lots of little Corys running around ready to turn up to claim their inheritance at any moment! "

"That's typical of you, Ariadnê," he replied, not hiding his disdain for his sister's harsh comments. "If you knew me, you would know that I always respected girls. Would you talk about *màna* with so much venom in your tone? She became pregnant with you before she was married, so don't throw insults around when you never met the girl in question."

"That's different and you know it," his sister argued. "How can you know a girl in just a couple of weeks? The whole situation is insane."

Cory had no answers to placate any of his family. *How can I explain to them that I know I was the person to take Adele's virginity?* he thought sadly. "All the dates are right," he told them. "Rodi was born on my birthday, nine months after I slept with her mother. Rodi's baby is named after me and also shares the same birthday."

"Coincidence," Ariadnê spat.

"Yes I know, but it could be because we are all of the same genes. Maybe some kind of blood test will tell us if we are related." He looked questioningly at Jacinta.

"There is something known as DNA testing, but it isn't widely available yet," she explained. "Blood tests are easy, but are often inconclusive and in this case unless Rodi knows her mother's blood group, it would be virtually impossible to prove parentage."

Cory looked around at his family. "I intend to get to the bottom of this," he told them. "You will all have to trust me. If I am a father, I would hope you would welcome my child into the family. If I'm not, then the problem is solved for us all."

"Not for the girl, Cory," Ariadnê said bluntly. "If you aren't her father, her problems start all over again and in all honesty, I can't say I care."

"That's uncalled for, Ariadnê," Eleni scolded. "We all have to support Cory in this. As a mother, I feel for the girl and I feel for my son." She stood and gave Cory a hug. "Don't worry. I'm here if and when you need me. I quite like the idea of having a granddaughter, not to mention a great-grandson," she said and then whispered, "Ignore your sister. She's always got her own agenda in everything. We are used to her sounding off. She'll come round in the end."

"Thanks, *Màna*. I knew I could count on you."

Twenty-nine

Rodi delivered a copy of Adele's codicil and her journal to the Demetriou residence as requested. She left the package in the mailbox while they were at work and then returned to St Kilda with hope in her heart.

"I have no idea how long he will take to read them," she told Jake on her return. "I gave him the telephone number of this place so hopefully he will call when he would like to see me again. I feel a bit in limbo now."

"I think we should start exploring Victoria a bit. We are here for another two months and we need to see some of this vast country while we are here," Jake suggested. "The rent is paid on this place, so it's our home away from home. We can stay overnight in places; make a proper holiday of our time here."

"But what if Demetriou calls while we're away?" Rodi asked plaintively. "He might think I'm not bothered about him if I'm not here to receive his call."

Jake sighed. "Rodi, he already knows you care about him by travelling thousands of miles to find him. We can't sit around waiting. He might take weeks to digest all that he has to read. If it will make you feel any better, we'll leave a message on his answering machine to tell him we'll be away in the Dandenongs for a week or so. I really fancy going up into the hills. The brochure shows some stunning pictures."

"All right…" She was interrupted by loud knocking on the door. "Who on earth can this be?" she said as Jake went to see who was almost banging the door down.

The woman barged in unceremoniously. She scanned the room, her eyes darting back and forth as she walked around as though she owned the place.

"Are you the owner?" Jake asked while Rodi stood mesmerised by the woman's intrusive manner.

"No I'm not," she said forcefully. "I'm Ariadnê Valli, Cory Demetriou's sister."

"Oh, how are you?" Rodi asked and went to shake her hand. "I'm so pleased to meet you."

Ariadnê did not offer her hand to return the friendly gesture. She stood her ground, arms akimbo and she looked directly at Rodi. "I don't know what you think you are doing, young lady, but I advise you to leave my brother alone. You come here uninvited, upsetting our family and making your claims. How do you know he's your father? Your mother could have made it up because she fancied him while on holiday. I used to see all the little English girls fluttering their eyelashes at our Greek boys. Fast cats, the lot of them." Her words were harsh, vicious.

Jake went to stand by his wife who appeared to be dumbstruck by this invasion of their privacy. "Look, Mrs Valli," he said quietly, yet confidently. "We have no argument with you. Indeed, we have no argument with any of your family. Our business is with your brother and it will only be discussed with *him* at this point. He has not told us to leave him alone and I really don't understand why you feel it necessary to speak on his behalf. I cannot believe he sent you. Our dealings with him so far have been extremely amicable and we trust he will deal with the situation how he finds appropriate."

"He's too kind. Always wants to be nice. He needs me to fight his battles for him. Go back to England; forget about this little game you are playing; just leave him alone," she said, strangely more calmly now.

Just at that moment, baby Cory woke from his nap. Rodi said, "Excuse me," and went to pick him up from his cot. She returned to the lounge room with the child in her arms.

Ariadnê visibly paled at the sight of him, but said nothing.

Rodi found her voice. "Mrs Valli, we haven't come all this way to cause trouble. Please understand that when your brother and I have discussed the situation and brought it to a conclusion for us both, my husband and I will return to Corfu—not to England as you suggested, because our home is on the beautiful island of your birth. Thank you for calling and making us aware of your feelings. Perhaps we will meet again in more favourable circumstances. Goodbye."

Ariadnê stepped forward slowly and stroked the baby's toes gently. She smiled at the child, shook her head slowly and left without another word.

Jake looked at Rodi in wonder. "What on earth was all that about?" he asked.

"I think she is questioning my motives in a big way," Rodi said with new confidence in her tone, "and who would blame her? I have to be prepared for some backlash from his family and that performance just now started out as an absolute humdinger!"

Jake breathed in deeply and expelled the air forcefully through pursed lips. "I'm proud of you, babe. When we started this search, I never thought I'd see the day when you would stand up for yourself like that. Every breakthrough and setback had you in tears previously, but not today. You had her in the palm of your hand before she left."

"Cory did, not me," she told him. "Did you see the look on her face when I brought him into the room?"

Jake slowly shook his head. "I can't say I noticed particularly."

"She recognised the family likeness, I know she did. She didn't have to say anything; I felt it. Any mother would. Maybe our child looks like his grandfather as a child. Who knows, but if her expression is anything to go by, I think we have made an ally even if she doesn't realise it at the moment. She definitely saw something, or somebody, in our child. That can only be to our advantage."

Jake gave her a hug. "Call the store and leave a message for your dad. Tell him we'll be back in a couple of weeks," Jake advised her. "That will give him time to go through your documents with a fine tooth comb. Ask to see him on our return. Let's pack our bags and go into the hills."

Thirty

Cory looked at the package and left it on the kitchen counter. Jacinta was working the night shift and he was alone. He picked at his dinner and looked at the package again. *What are you afraid of?* he asked himself silently. *Do you think the truth is going to make you happy, or will you be disappointed? Do you want Rodi Saunders to be your daughter?* He wrestled with his thoughts and picked up the package. Holding it to his heart, he wished for the wisdom to deal with what was to come. *Just do it,* he told himself firmly. *You have to know one way or another.*

He opened the envelope carefully as if protecting its contents. Considering which he ought to read first, he glanced at the sheets of paper that were part of Adele's last will and testament and he shuddered at the thought that his first true love had gone forever. *I can never tell her that I loved her dearly, that she left a heart longing for her love and a body yearning for her touch. I can't tell her I didn't love again until Jacinta showed me how.* "I didn't abandon you, my dear, sweet Adele. I waited and waited..." he cried and then he began reading.

My dearest wish is that my daughter, Aphrodite (Rodi by her own volition) finds her father, Cory Demetriou, last known to me at the Hotel Helenya, near Paleokastritsa on the island of Corfu in August 1959. She has the right to know him as I never did. There is no animosity; I fell in love with him when I was on holiday. I have no regrets and she has been the perfect daughter, but I owe it to her to allow her to know her father and hopefully discover the handsome, charming and caring man I met and loved albeit for a very short time. Kalí týchi, Rodi.

Dear Adele, she even learned a bit of Greek. He smiled at the thought.

Why should he consider I would be different to the other girls he met? English girls on holiday on the romantic island of Corfu never considered the consequences of holiday flings. He never wrote to me and because of that I have to accept it was just a holiday romance for him, but it was the time I fell hopelessly in love, the only time I had been completely in love. He was the most handsome man I had ever seen, but probably had hundreds of holiday romances every summer, so why would I be any different to the others?

No, no, Adele. You are wrong! I told you when we were together. Didn't you believe me? It was you who never wrote to me after the postcard. I kept on writing until my letters were returned unopened and I had to find the courage to accept you no longer wanted me. He sighed deeply and continued to read.

When my parents bundled me off to St Vincent's, I received no letters at all. Maybe my stepmother threw away my mail...she was always prone to do something like that, but I will never know.

Oh sweet Adele, it must have been your stepmother who returned the letters to me. She obviously had no intentions of allowing me to be a part of yours or your baby's lives.

I had to resign myself to the fact that the love of my life would never know he was about to become a father. I didn't want to write to him again for fear of rejection. Teenagers dreaded being rejected by a boy and I was no different. Common sense told me not to bombard him with letters and I didn't want him to deny our love when I laid fatherhood at his door. I had too much to think about to get through my pregnancy. I was sixteen years old, alone and about to produce a child I knew I would love until the end of my days. My best friend Eva would have helped if she had received my letters to her, but her mother intercepted them and told me never to contact Eva again. A pregnant teenager was not socially accepted by many people at that time.

Cory felt tears trickle down his cheeks and he didn't brush them away. Doing so would be like pushing Adele and her child away again and he knew he wouldn't do that. "Oh my goodness," he said out loud. *Even Eva deserted her... I remember Eva well. I want to believe all this. Adele told me she had a boyfriend at home, but assured me it wasn't serious. How can I really know I was the only one who made love to her? I am so confused. Why can't I just accept what she is saying? There has to be something which will convince me,* he thought earnestly.

> *Now that I know I am going to die, I have to make sure that Rodi knows her father. I have always kept it a secret from her. Only my parents knew and they passed away before Rodi was old enough to understand. I have no way of convincing anybody I only made love with a man twice in my life and both those occasions were with Cory Demetriou in Corfu in 1959. I only hope there will be something in my final words that will convince him I am speaking the truth. I know I am giving my beloved daughter a mammoth challenge, but she deserves to know who she is, where she came from and understand she was a product of true love. Should she be successful in meeting her father, I would ask that he looks into her eyes. There he will see me. Please give her the love of the father she deserves. I truly loved you, Cory. Gia pánta tin agápi. Forever love.*

Cory lay back on the sofa and sobbed. He felt wretched. His heart was aching because of what he had not known. He remembered his love for Adele as if it were yesterday, but he had overcome his grief of losing her and had learned to love again. *I do love Jacinta,* he convinced himself silently, *but I loved Adele then and I cannot deny that. I want to believe what she writes is true, but there is something nagging at me to dig deeper into it to find undeniable evidence not just for me, but for everybody concerned.*

When Jacinta returned from work the following morning, she noted that Cory was pale. Dark rings under his eyes told her he'd had a restless night. "Can I do anything to help, sweetheart?" she asked before he went to work.

"Not really," he replied. "I started reading Adele's will last night. Pretty heart-felt stuff. I couldn't help but be moved by it."

Jacinta reached out and rubbed his arm affectionately. "Does it make things any clearer for you?"

"Not really. It just made me relive the time we were together…" He paused poignantly as he saw what he interpreted as hurt in Jacinta's eyes. "Darling Jacinta," he assured her. "You have no need to be worried. I have always been honest with you and you know the love I share with you now is not like the love I shared with Adele. Ours is mature love, constant and true, strong and lasting. If Rodi is my daughter, I hope you will accept her into our family. I would like you to meet her anyway. I know you will see her for the lovely young woman she has become. Daughter or not, I know I have made friends of her and Jake." He took her into his arms and held her tightly.

"I don't feel threatened anymore, Cory," she said quietly. "I am sure of your love for me, but I think you will be disappointed if Rodi isn't your daughter after all." She smiled affectionately. "I'm here for you, darling, and for Rodi, too, if she needs me."

"That's all I need to hear," he said and he kissed her on the forehead. "Now I need to go to work and you need to get some sleep. I'll be home before you leave for work this evening."

Cory was surprised by his eagerness to start reading Rodi's journal. He felt more comfortable now that Jacinta had given her approval and he ate dinner quickly so that he could settle down for the evening to read what he thought would be an interesting book.

18 March 1981- As I start writing this journal, I have no idea what destiny holds in store for me. I am setting out on a journey to find my father whom I have never known and who knows nothing of my existence. I don't know how many mountains I shall have to climb, or how hazardous my journey will be, but I owe it to my mum, who alone has raised me, and come hell or high water, I shall carry out her last wish for her and for me. I am on a plane flying to Corfu, the land of my conception in the hope that my father, Cory Demetriou is still there.

Cory shifted in his chair. His thoughts were already in a whirl. *The poor girl was going on a wild goose chase. Almost six years ago now and I was long gone. She obviously had so much faith in her mother. Why can't I return the compliment when I loved Adele dearly?*

He returned to his reading.

Mum never mentioned Cory Demetriou to me. Maybe she preferred to forget, but I hope she wasn't sad because of having loved and lost. Dear Mum; she protected me all my life from the details of my father. I'm sad about that. I wonder if she were ashamed? She told me my name came from her love of Greek mythology.

Cory shivered involuntarily.

I never even knew my father was Greek. She only ever told me that she had fallen in love—once—and I was the product of that love. When I asked where my father was, she always said she didn't know and asked me not to talk about him. Out of love and respect for her, I did as she asked, but now...

Cory found it fascinating. He found the dedication and commitment inspirational and he felt like an intruder as he read of Rodi leaving her boyfriend in England and then meeting Jake. By allowing him to read her journal, she had made him an unwilling party to their first love-making when they were in Thessaloniki. He was awed by the fact they had tried to find Yannis Papakostas in Lakones and he was disgusted as he learned of the antics of Roussos, the barman. *Very like his uncle,* he thought. *Marcos Roussos always liked to cause problems for others.* He sighed. *So many memories in here for me. They even found Antonis, who helped them. God bless him; such a dear friend...'*

When Jacinta returned home, he was much brighter than he had been the previous day. "It's like reading my biography," he told her. "They have found out so much about me. They even went to my old college and the hotel where I worked. I had to stop reading at midnight because my eyes were tired. It's quite fascinating, Jacinta. They have gone to such great lengths to trace me."

"They certainly appear to be determined in their efforts," she agreed, "but is it helping you?"

He breathed in deeply and looked sad. "If I'm honest, I am thinking maybe I am Rodi's father, because I cannot believe that anybody would travel so far over a long period and spend so much money on trying to find me if it weren't true, but..."

"Ah, there's a *but,* is there?" Jacinta asked curiously.

"Unfortunately, yes," he conceded. "They are doing this all on Adele's say-so. Much as I want to trust her and I hate myself for not doing so, I desperately need something more before I can embrace Rodi Saunders as my daughter."

Thirty-one

When Rodi and Jake returned to St Kilda, they were disappointed that there was no news from Demetriou. "He's had two whole weeks to read my journal and Mum's will. How long does he need?" Rodi said, exasperated with the lack of communication.

"You're doing it again, Rodi," Jake said smiling at his wife.

"Doing what?"

"Opening your mouth without thinking it through," he explained gently. "Put yourself in his shoes. He works long hours and he has a wife with whom he will want to spend quality time when they've been working all day. When you had time off, would you want to be reading documents which might contain information that will disrupt your life forever?"

Rodi pressed her lips together in a straight line. Her eyes were sad. "But I *know* he is my father," she said with heartfelt emotion in her voice. "Why can't he see it too?"

"How do you know, babe?" Jake asked.

"I know because I knew my mum. She wouldn't make it up. Why should she?" she said earnestly.

Jake sighed and went to sit next to his wife who was holding Cory on her lap. His little feet were kicking merrily and as he chortled, Jake stroked his toes tenderly. "I love his toes," he said. "Babies' feet are always so cute."

Rodi laughed. "I know and he has the tiny web between his little pinkie and the one next to it just like me. It must run..." She stopped suddenly and both she and Jake simultaneously recognised the revelation that presented itself to them. "That's it!" she exclaimed. "Mum often said she wondered where I had got that from. Her feet weren't like mine at all. If Demetriou's feet are like ours, it might be the proof he needs. Do you think I should call him?"

Just then the telephone rang. "Jake Saunders," he said as he picked up the receiver.

"Jake, hi, it's Cory Demetriou." His voice was low.

"What a coincidence," Jake told him. "We were just about to call you. We have some additional news..."

"Keep it until we see you," Demetriou said abruptly. "I would like you to meet my wife. She has some time off and I'm taking time off too. We would like to invite you to our place on Saturday so that we might spend some time together, perhaps get to know each other a little better."

"That's very kind of you both. Thank you," Jake said amicably. "Did you manage to read the documents?"

"I did and I would like to talk about the contents with you both on Saturday. There is too much to discuss over the phone," Demetriou explained seriously.

"Okay," Jake said feeling a little deflated. "I hope everything is all right."

"Nothing we can't deal with," Demetriou said, but Jake noticed a lack of enthusiasm in his voice.

"We'll see you on Saturday then. What time would you like us to arrive?"

Demetriou was silent for a moment. "Sorry about the delay," he said. "I was just asking Jacinta what time. Come in time for morning tea—elevenses I think, for you Poms."

Jake laughed. "Yes, you're correct. We'll be there for eleven o'clock then. Can we bring anything?"

"Just bring yourselves. We'll have morning tea and a light lunch," Demetriou told him. "My extended family will come later for dinner. We hope little Cory will be all right to stay so long."

"He'll be fine," Jake assured him. "He'll sleep in his pushchair when he is tired, so no problem. Thank you again. We'll see you on Saturday."

"We'll look forward to it," Demetriou told him. "*Zíto*."

"*Zíto*, Cory. Cheerio," Jake replied, proud that he had displayed his linguistic ability, albeit very basic.

Rodi was pacing the floor all the time Jake was on the phone. "What did he say?" she asked eagerly. "He obviously wants to see us. I picked that up as you were talking."

Jake looked puzzled. "He's sending mixed messages," he said.

"How?" Rodi asked curiously.

"He said he'd read the will and the journal, but he gave no hint of his feelings about them. In fact, he sounded rather unenthusiastic and didn't want to discuss anything over the phone. Then he said he wanted his wife to meet us and later for us to meet his whole family. Seems odd to me."

"Oh dear," Rodi said despondently. "That doesn't sound good at all."

"But why would he want to spend the whole day with us and want us to meet his family?" Jake asked.

"Could be he wants them to back up his views, especially if they are negative," Rodi declared. "Look at his sister. She didn't inspire me with confidence at all. Maybe she's spread her opinion around the rest of the Demetrious. Who knows?"

Ever the pragmatist, Jake offered his immediate thoughts on the situation. "Let's not anticipate things we don't know. We can take heart from the fact that they want to spend time with us. We can see how things go and then ask about..." He paused and grinned. "...about little toes if and when necessary."

~ * ~

Rodi's nerves were on edge when Saturday came. "I'm scared, Jake," she said when they were driving to South Yarra. "I so much need this to have a positive outcome."

"So do I," Jake said to reassure her of his support, "but we have to think sensibly about it. We have been successful in finding Cory Demetriou. You have already carried out your mum's wishes. She didn't say anything about him having to accept you as his daughter."

"She didn't have to say it, Jake," Rodi argued. "She actually left a message for him in the codicil, didn't she? Something about looking into my eyes and seeing her. That means she hoped he would admit his part in all this."

"Don't bank on anything," he warned her. "We can't make him believe what we have presented to him. He has to be completely happy to admit paternity. If he rejects your claims as his sister did, there is little more we can do except play the little toe card." He smiled warmly. "I never realised how important little toes could be."

"Maybe his little toes are normal," Rodi said light-heartedly. "In that case, I can't do anything else to convince him. It's in the lap of the gods, Greek ones of course, but I do feel more relaxed now just talking to you about it. 'What will be will be'."

They pulled up at the house at five minutes to eleven. "Good timing, or what?" Jake gloated as he parked the car on the driveway.

They lifted Cory out of the baby car seat and allowed him to walk to the door. "Good boy, Cory," Rodi said to the child. "You are a big boy, aren't you? Come on, Mummy will lift you up so you can ring the bell."

"Bell! Bell!" the child cried excitedly. "Ting-a-ling, Mummy!"

Demetriou answered the door almost immediately. "Welcome," he said with a smile.

Jake in particular noticed how like Rodi he was. *That smile has convinced me,* he thought. *It's almost as disarming as Rodi's was when I first set eyes on her. I wonder if Jacinta will see the same thing in Rodi?*

Rodi could feel marauding butterflies in her stomach, but she tried desperately not to let her nervousness show. She handed him the wine and chocolates they had brought for their hosts. "We couldn't come empty handed," she told him. "How are you?" Her thoughts were running riot in her head. *I don't even know what to call him. Mr Demetriou seems so formal and yet Cory is too familiar. Maybe I'll just avoid giving him a name.*

The whole of the ground floor was an open plan and Jacinta was behind the kitchen counter when they entered. She smiled and said, "*Geia. Ti kánete?* Oh sorry, I should speak English. I forget when I am at home."

Rodi smiled and replied, "*Geia. Eímai efcharistó polý. Ti kánete?* My Greek is very limited, but I keep on trying. Maybe when we go back to Corfu, I shall try harder." She glanced around the room which integrated kitchen, dining area and family room. "You have a lovely home."

Jacinta appeared to be taken aback. "Thank you and in response to your Greek, you are doing well," she said.

As if responding to Rodi's earlier quandary, Jake asked Demetriou, "What do we call you? We now have two Corys in our presence. It could get confusing. Cory Senior?"

Demetriou laughed heartily. "That makes me sound ancient," he said in good humour. "Please try Cory. I don't think the baby will respond to adult conversation." He said it with a wink and his friendliness was noted particularly by Jake. "Shall we sit on the terrace? The river looks lovely today. Coffee? Or perhaps you would prefer tea?"

Rodi laughed. "In spite of what you might have heard about the English, we do drink coffee for elevenses and tea in the afternoon," she told them light-heartedly.

"Coffee it is then," Jacinta said. "How do you like it?"

"Flat white with one, please," Rodi told her. "Both of us the same."

"Right. Do take a seat outside and I'll bring it out to you in a moment."

Having drunk their coffee, Jake suggested he would walk around with baby Cory and try to get him to sleep. "It's time for his nap, so I'll leave you to it."

Rodi thanked him and Jacinta diplomatically went to prepare lunch.

There was an awkward pause in the conversation then Demetriou broke the silence. "You met Tia Giannopoulos, I believe."

Rodi took a quick breath. *Here we go,* she thought. "I did and how fortuitous it was," she told him. "We wouldn't be sitting here now but for Tia. She was very helpful."

"And to me too," Demetriou said. "I can't say I would never have found my family but for her, because Jacinta and I were planning to emigrate anyway. Tia just helped to confirm we had made the right decision. Nice girl. We were college friends."

"So I believe," Rodi said not knowing how to react. Tia had divulged she liked Demetriou in college, but the feelings weren't reciprocated.

"I'm pleased she's happy in Corfu," he said amicably. He took a deep breath. "You and I have some serious talking to do, don't we?"

"We do," she agreed, "and I have to admit I'm very nervous."

"Me too," Demetriou admitted. "I guess we had better be honest with each other so that neither of us is under any illusions."

Rodi's heart sank. "I have never been anything but honest," she assured him.

"I know that, Rodi," he said warmly, "and having read what your mother wrote in her will, I have to say she brought back a lot of memories for me." He paused and took Rodi's hand. "I loved her. In the short time we had together, she made me feel loved, wanted and very special."

Rodi felt tears welling in her eyes. "You have no idea how good that makes me feel," she said.

"I didn't love again until I met Jacinta. That's how much effect Adele had on me. I thought she had broken my heart, but it seems I broke hers too," he continued. "I'm sorry, but when my letters to her were returned unopened, I had to presume the worst. I thought she just considered I was a holiday romance and nothing more."

"She always told me she loved you very much, but she didn't know where you were," Rodi told him, holding on to his hand for the security she needed. "I can only think she must have been in the unmarried mothers' home when your letters arrived and her stepmother returned them. She and her stepmother didn't see eye-to-eye as far as I can gather. I think you and I both have to believe that's what happened."

"I agree," he said, "but whilst I admit everything that happened between your mother and me, I still have a nagging doubt that I may not be your father."

Rodi was momentarily stunned. "May I ask why?"

Cory held on to her hand and explained. "Adele had a boyfriend at home. She told me about him and said it was nothing serious. How can I possibly know if she slept with him, or not? I want to believe you are my daughter, Rodi. I feel it in my heart, but my head is telling me not to trust my emotions. Jacinta told me we could have blood tests, but they are often inconclusive and if we don't know your mother's blood group, I think we might be wasting our time."

"I don't know her blood group at all," Rodi admitted, her manner clearly displaying her despair. "I'll try to find out, but it will mean going to England and it will take ages. Just at the moment, I feel I will die if we can't settle this before Jake and I return to Corfu." She sighed deeply and the tears trickled down her cheeks again.

Demetriou leaned forward and wiped her tears away with gentle fingers. "Please don't cry, baby," he said affectionately.

Rodi sniffed and took a deep breath. "I do understand what you are saying and I would never put pressure on you to say you are sure about being my father, but I know my mother wouldn't lie. She was the most honest and genuine person I've ever known. Even Eva said that when we met at Hotel Helenya."

"I don't know what else to say to help to solve the problem," he said. "I see Adele in your eyes. You both have the most beautiful blue eyes."

"Thank you," she managed to say through her tears.

Suddenly loud voices were heard. "We're here! Can we come in?"

"Oh," Demetriou said. "Is it that time already? This will be my family. Are you all right, or shall I ask them to wait in the lounge room?"

Rodi took a tissue and dried her eyes. "I'm fine," she said. "I'm looking forward to meeting them. I'll just find Jake and Cory and we'll be right in."

She found Jake with his feet dangling in the pool and the baby chortling in his pushchair. "So this is what you get up to when I'm not around?" she asked to hide her distress.

"Baby, what's the matter?" Jake asked, seeing the desperation on her face.

"Later," she told him. "We need to put on a brave face and meet the family. Come on. We don't want to be rude."

~ * ~

"Rodi and Jake, meet my mother, Eleni and my stepfather, Cyrus."

"Pleased to meet you," they said cordially.

"We are pleased to meet you too," Eleni said, "and who's this little fellow?" she asked as she peeped round the hood of the pushchair to find Cory. "Oh my goodness!" she exclaimed. "Ariadnê was right."

"What do you mean Ariadnê was right?" Demetriou asked. "I haven't seen her since they got back from holidaying on the Gold Coast. What are you talking about?"

Rodi felt uncomfortable. She had said nothing about Ariadnê's visit.

Eleni called her daughter in from the lounge room. "Come in here and explain to your brother what you told me," she called.

Ariadnê came in looking sheepish. "I did something I am ashamed of," she said quietly.

"Case of brain, mouth and actions not being in sync again," her husband announced to the family who had gathered on the terrace.

Jake smiled. "That's you all over," he whispered affectionately to his wife.

Ariadnê continued. "I called at the Saunders' place before we went on holiday."

"You did what?" her brother asked astonished at her audacity.

"I'm sorry. I thought I was doing the family a favour," she explained, "but when I saw little Cory, I was amazed. He is the absolute image of you as a baby, dear brother! There is no way you can deny being his grandfather."

Demetriou gasped. "How can you be so sure?" he asked, irritated that his sister was intimating he should accept his paternity on her say-so.

Ariadnê ignored his query. She moved towards the pushchair. "May I pick him up?" she asked Rodi, who nodded to give her approval. "Come on, little one. We have something to prove you and I." She removed her shoes. "Take off your shoes, Cory," she demanded.

"What?"

"Take off your shoes. Everybody," she instructed, "look at our feet. Our little toes are attached to the adjoining toe with a little web. It is inherited from our father—God rest his soul. It isn't very visible to everybody else, but we know it is there."

Rodi began to remove her sandals and she smiled broadly at Jake.

"Look at this child's beautiful little toes," Ariadnê instructed.

Demetriou gasped as Rodi too planted her feet among those displayed by the Demetriou family.

Cory Demetriou cupped his daughter's face in his hands and kissed her on both cheeks. "My baby," he said through his tears. "My own special baby."

Applause and hugs welcomed Rodi, Jake and Cory into the family. There were lots of tears and smiles. Rodi could only say, "Thank you. Thank you from the bottom of my heart."

"Please excuse me a moment," Demetriou said and he disappeared upstairs. When he reappeared, he was carrying a little wooden dog on wheels. "I have kept this since I was a child and it has gone everywhere with me—Athens, Cyprus and now Australia. It has been my keepsake from my childhood, but will you allow me to give it to Cory?" he asked.

"Bow-wow!" the child exclaimed with glee and held out his chubby hand to his namesake.

"If you are sure you want to part with such a valuable part of your past," Rodi said, "I'm sure Cory would love it."

"Bow-wow!" the child said again and took the cord that was the leash by which he might pull the little dog around.

Jacinta was amused. "What is bow-wow?" she asked.

Jake explained. "Baby talk for dog in the UK. It supposedly sounds like the dog's bark. It looks like our little boy loves it already. Thank you, *Pappous*."

Grandad smiled with pride. "I like that," he said. "I like being a *pappous* very much."

Baby Cory walked round and round pulling the little dog behind him. "He's made a friend," Jake joked. "He'll never let go now. You watch. He'll keep hold of it all day and I'm sure it will find a way into his bed tonight!"

As they watched baby Cory playing with his new toy, *Pappous* produced a bundle of letters tied together with thin blue cord. He handed them to Rodi. "Read those when you have time," he instructed. "They contain the proof that I loved your mother and you will find photographs of us together. You allowed me the privilege of sharing your most personal moments during your search. I would like you to share my moments with your mother."

Rodi looked at Jacinta to gain her permission and approval.

"It's all good, Rodi. I will never take the place of your mother, but I would like you to be a part of my life with your father." Jacinta smiled affectionately at her new stepdaughter.

Later they sat around the dinner table and enjoyed their first family meal together. Raising his glass, Grandad Cory made a toast. "To Adele. Thank you for having the wisdom to bring us all together."

Glasses clinked. "To Adele."

Meet
Vera Berry Burrows

Vera Berry-Burrows is a UK-born former teacher of English Language and Literature, living in Queensland, Australia with journalist husband, Alan. She has a son and two grandsons living in the UK. She has been writing for a number of years and has had numerous non-fiction articles published in the UK and in Australia. She was educated at Farnworth Grammar School in Lancashire, trained as a teacher at St Katharine's College, Liverpool and gained a Bachelor of Arts degree with the Open University.

Since she took early retirement in 1994 having been in the teaching profession for thirty one years, writing has become her compulsive hobby.

Other Works From The Pen Of

Vera Berry Burrows

<u>Tomorrow Never Comes</u> - March 2011
Relationships seriously affect the lives of a controlling mother, Nell Winston and her rebellious son, Joel until the elusive tomorrows make all the earth-shattering yesterdays worthwhile.

<u>Regarding Kimberley</u> - February 2012
Kimberley Mason unwittingly unearths a thirty year old dark secret kept by her parents when she forms links with a theatrical agency in Sydney, Australia.

<u>Connections</u> - April 2013
Connections, for better or worse, made by Jane O'Connell after divorce, completely disrupt her life, both shattering and illuminating her existence with unexpected consequences.

<u>Family Matters</u> -October 2013
In war-torn Britain, John Hawthorne and three daughters, Meg, Patty and Abigail, rally forth on the battlefield of their own shattered lives.

A Message to Our Readers

Enjoy this book?

You can make a difference.

As an independent publisher, Wings ePress, Inc. does not have the financial clout of the large New York publishers. We can't afford large magazine spreads or subway posters to tell people about our quality books.

But we do have something much more effective and powerful than ads. We have a large base of loyal readers.

Honest reviews help bring the attention of new readers to our books.

If you enjoyed this book, we would appreciate it if you would spend a few minutes posting a review on the site where you purchased this book or on the Wings ePress, Inc. webpages at:

https://wingsepress.com/

Thank You